MW01226636

POWER SOURCE

BOOK TWO: WOLF IN THE FOLD

VINCE REED

OcT. 2012

PublishAmerica
Baltimore

First printing

All characters in this book are fictitious, and any resemblance to real persons, living or dead, is coincidental.

PublishAmerica has allowed this work to remain exactly as the author intended, verbatim, without editorial input.

Softcover 9781462697106
PUBLISHED BY PUBLISHAMERICA, LLLP
www.publishamerica.com
Baltimore

Printed in the United States of America

To my brother Mike,
for helping me
dream "The Dream."

Excerpt from Power Source—Book One:

The first atomic bomb was tested in 1945 during World War II. Our government called it the "Manhattan Project". It is said that some of the scientists who developed such a devastating instrument of death did so thoroughly believing that such a creation would finally bring peace to the war driven world because of the fear of using it even once, that the mere existence of such a conception would scare our planet into examining for more peaceful solutions to the differences that grew between us. Little were the scientists aware that their government had different ideas, as eventually even more devastating tools of destruction would be developed by not only their own country, but others that soon followed around the globe.

Occasionally, throughout the fragile thread of time, it is bestowed on someone to carry the mantle of making a critical decision. An epiphany is set, a choice has to be made that will change the course of a people, a country, or even a world forever. For those who make such a decision and being completely unaware of the tremendous impact their choice will have, I have often envied. But for those who are keenly aware of the full bearing that their choice will have on their fellow humans around them and the full and permanent impression it will have on their world, the burden is heavy, and often too arduous for any one person to carry alone.

There are individuals in our little world who currently obsess themselves with finding solutions to our current problem of dwindling fossil fuels, while others feed ferociously on the rivalry and confrontation, trying to achieve dominion over the remaining resources, thus creating yet another excuse to maintain the war like attitude that seems to be ever prevalent throughout Earth's history.

I am one of the former. During all this conflict and turmoil, I had made a prodigious discovery of my own. I had found a solution to an idea that I had been working on, these last few years, all while being employed by our own government in the area of advancing the ability of our country to destroy an enemy in the name of maintaining world peace. Or it would be more accurate to state that; the discovery found me. While spending some precious, and personal time on the open sea, on my father's yacht somewhere within the in the Polynesian anthology of islands, I happened on an uncharted sea mount. And there, I found a small sample of a yet unknown mineral which held within it such faculty and power as the world has never known.

The epiphany. For as I was discovering its power to turn the world's energy problem forever, along with many more things did I realized it would do for the benefit of mankind, I had also found that it could, and would, be used for such destruction as was never known since that first atomic test. Right then I made a choice.

While the mineral itself, being the root of my discoveries, remained known only to me, the government in which I worked knew of my success generally and wanted total hegemony. As my experiments advanced to include things like automobiles, and ultimately aircraft, others holding power in the commercial world, becoming attentive to my breakthroughs, also wanted to get their hands on my discoveries either to suppress the knowledge or to advance themselves in their own financial might.

Their quest for what I knew, and the battles that ensued, drove me deeper into isolation, as well as to trigger even more fantastic innovations, as eventually I found the ultimate solution to the mounting impasse. And all of this due to the mineral which I have dubbed; "Polynesium".

PROLOGUE

It had changed their lives forever and they were bound to protect this powerful secret, no matter what, even with their lives if they had to. Now It appeared that they would be on the run forever, battling not only their own government but now other governments, as well as many of the private sector around the globe who hungered for what could be the world's greatest source of power ever! As this newly found, and extremely rare, resource unfolded more and more fantastic innovations for Nelsson and Cooper, the battle to keep their formidable discoveries hidden was almost lost when one day their ultimate dream was finally realized as both now head for the stars in what would be Earth's first interstellar spacecraft!

Driven by the turmoil that was wrought by the innovations that the mineral, Nelsson had dubbed polynesium, had produced, they venture off seeking peace at last, away from their own warmongering, power hungry planet only to be driven further by the haunting dreams that had been plaguing Nelsson for some time. Obsessed in finding the cause of his visions they stumble on a planet far more advanced then Earth. The discovery of polynesium and its power was, as of yet, still unknown to these so called peace loving people, but the Pasarin's had a big secret of their own, and as a consequence, Nelsson and Cooper find themselves, yet again, in a battle for ascendancy, which eventually led them to discovering the source of Nelsson's disturbing dreams which will ultimately give him the shock of his life!

CHAPTER ONE

EXPOSURE

Jumbled Images flowed and ebbed. The visions surged and shaped themselves into meaningless metaphors from times past as I tried to grab onto some sort of rational thought pattern among the sea of visualizations replaying events that still haunted me. A lot has happened. Maybe too much, and it possessed even my deepest emotions creating an impression of life now stained with distrust and suspicion. I had always sot peace at this time, being my only escape from the turmoil that followed me, but it would now seem to pursue me even to the deepest recesses of my being.

As I was thus battling my subconscious in the attempt to achieve some sort of reconciliation, the imagery slowly enclosed around me, shrouding me with a new reality. Completely forgetting all else, I now accepted my current state as actual, notwithstanding the lack of authenticity of any genuineness but totally accepting what I now experienced as sincere. My hidden stage was now set and I began to play out my part with in, despite the fact that it kept changing and refiguring itself as new emotions and reflections continued to color the counterfeit surroundings complete with its artificial characters each performing their assigned parts in the drama. Time was inconsequential now and had no part in the spectacle as the forged recreations jumped from thought to thought and from sensation to sensation dragging me helplessly along with it.

Without warning, the visions became far more vivid and a great deal sharper than before, suddenly increasing with varied intensity. It was as though I had been suddenly transported to some unexplainable realm by an unseen force that had, somehow, taken control of my thoughts even down to the very center. A new arena unfolded and quickly began to play out similes, in my mind, that I had never seen or ever could have imagined on my own before. Images and flashes of a people, never before supposed, appeared before my eyes. Buildings and structures the style of which have never been perceived, formed around them. The manifestations appeared to be that of antiquity. But nothing out of history matched what I was witnessing. No book, that I knew of, had ever recorded such a people or place, thus being unable to identify what I saw at all, even so, I continued to absorb the revelations as they came. So very strange yet, somehow familiar. The language was not any that I had ever heard either and yet sometimes I believed I understood it, or at least felt that I did. As the representation engaged itself round about me, I found myself unable to carry out any of my own will inside it. It was as if I was a puppet in someone else's play, a simple reflection in somebody else's mind, a mere rider on another's notion, being carried along like a leaf in a powerful stream. I was being controlled to do, and speak at someone else's whim. My curiosity and fascination began to turn to fear, as I struggled to take control, but, the more effort I gave to have power over my surroundings, the more ensnared and confined I became. My fear turned to panic as helplessness swallowed any hope of escaping my strange, and yet fantastic confinement.

While the impressions, that I was receiving, failed to carry out any manner of coherent sequence of events, what I did see became increasingly violent. Feelings of panic, fear, and anger flooded back to me like a torrent of water in a broken dam. Were these my feelings? Screaming! There was screaming, yelling, and fighting! A struggle. Several men pulling on another man. More screaming. I saw an older woman crying. And there, two younger women joining in the raucous, pulling and screaming. The vision waned for a moment then flooded back with a vengeance. More men came carrying some sort of rudimentary weapons. Crossbows?! I appeared to be deep in the brawl myself along with the girls and the older woman that I saw, doing my own share of pulling and scratching. Scratching? Was I screaming? It was me but not my voice that I heard. Female?! Then pain! Someone pulling my hair! My vision turned to look as then I saw one of the men pulling on a lock of long blond hair. My LONG BLOND hair!? I struggled, or at least my apparition did, as the vociferousness continued to flood the room and my senses. The crossbow. I found myself to be focused on it as it was suddenly fired at someone in the room.

In an instant all went dead quiet. I sat up in bed and breathed out slowly, covered in sweat, my head still spinning from the bits and pieces of the dream that remained. My room was dark and silent except for the air flow that quietly whispered from the ventilators. "Wow, that was wild." Relieved to hear my own voice coming out again, I turned around I looked out the window behind me, above my pillow. Uncountable stars gleamed back, all in their variety of sizes and intensity. Still there. All was silent.

Throwing the covers back I put my feet on the warm soft carpet and made my way to the bathroom. Sensing my presence, the door softly slid open as the room light suddenly flicked on. My feet found the cold bathroom floor bringing me out of my bewilderment and a little closer to reality. After giving myself some blatter relief, I walked over to the sink and glanced into the mirror as I washed. "Your definitely not getting any younger, old man." After a quick inspection to see if I, indeed, was getting some more gray, I wobbled back and sat down on my bed in dark. "Maxx, what time is it?" I asked the dark.

"Four hours, twenty three minutes, seventeen seconds," replied a male yet obviously electronic voice. With another sigh I Pulled my feet in the covers and began to get comfortable again. "Are you ok, sir?"

"Yes Maxx, I'm fine." How did that thing get so bloody personal? "Night mode please, Maxx." I would swear that its writing its own software. In fifteen minutes I was back to sleep.

*   *   *   *   *   *

"You're off your game, Skipper." George Cooper thought he finally had the upper hand on his captain. The two of us were battling it out in one of the several game rooms on deck four. Winning one of these would certainly put a notch in George's belt, and having something to hang over his captain's head would be sweet indeed, however George believed I was off my game in a much more important way.

"I think I'm going to go ahead and do it." I did my best to maintain my focus, although my mind seemed to be split into another thought. Large, steel broadswords smashed together again and again as we tested and sharpened each other's skills, something we try to do at least once a week. How we ever kept from mortally wounding each other was a miracle in itself, but this friendly yet dangerous form of belligerence had, over time, become one of the several ways we found in maintaining our sanity through all that brought us to this point in time. My companion's larger stature seemed to do very little in helping him out, however.

"What's that?" George prodded. "Yer gettin' married finally? He seemed to be swinging his sword a little rougher than usual. "Start socializing with real human beings instead of a ship full of holograms? You've been talking to Maxx too long my friend."

"We've been through this George." Annoyance with the same old conversation we've had too many times before was adding power to my own swing. "What would you have me do? Go back to earth and be shot at? To be put on trial for this thing and that thing over and over again? Have everybody on the planet clawing at me for what THEY think I've discovered or invented? Wanting me to do this for 'em, or to do that for 'em? To continue to be hunted like an animal and harassed by everybody from the government to who knows who, while being accused of everything under the sun, including being an alien from another planet? All while denying the very inventions they sought after. There'd be no peace. There WAS no peace." My hate for this particular subject was very evident as my next swing knocked the sword out of Mr. Cooper's hand.

"Ouch!" He quickly picked it up just in time for my next blow. "I understand that, I was there, remember? At some point you're going to have to break this wall down that you've created and learn to trust again 'ol buddy."

"I've got my kids," I responded with blows much harder now. "And am doing just fine. Besides you're human and you haven't exactly been goin' steady with anybody yourself there, Mr. Cooper." Backing George up against the wall, with a swing and a flick of my sword, I flipped George's sword up in the air causing it to stick to the wall close to the ceiling. "Rock n' Roll."

We stopped to catch our breath as I gave my partner a slap on the back. "One of the many little tricks our new friends taught me during my long stay."

"I hate it when you do that," He grunted breathlessly, shaking his hand. "One of these days I'm going to learn not to get you so stirred up."

"One day."

"It's not like I've had much of a chance going out on dates out here in the middle of space, ya know."

"Well, like wise. George, I appreciate what your trying to do. But I'm fine. I'm happy. Please…, no more 'you should get married again' speeches." I then tried to change the subject back to the original one. "Ya know, there's a bigger reason why the Pasarins don't want us to go to their, so called, planet of mystery." I hung my sword on the rack with the others as George simply stares at his, now too high on the wall to reach. "I figure it wouldn't hurt to take a small peek just to see what we could see." Leaving the game room we took our conversation out into the corridor.

"Hard to stay out of trouble?" George asked. "There's another reason why you're going, isn't there? Admit it."

"Maxx, do we have the location of this planet?" I asked.

"Affirmative," responded the computer from somewhere unseen. "The planet in which you are referring is on file."

"Set course, best speed, full cloak," I commanded.

"Acknowledge."

"What gives you the notion that this so called 'planet of mystery' will give you any answers?"

I walked toward the nearest elevator ignoring George's question.

"Those dreams are back, aren't they?" he barbed again. "Why don't you just admit that's why you're going? Why THAT planet? This is just another one of your wild goose chases, isn't it?"

"You're NOT giving me that 'you should get married' speech again! Like I said George, I know your trying to help, but I don't need a shrink. What is it with this ship? Why is everybody trying to marry me off? I'm happy, contented! I'm fine!"

"Ya know we've spend a lot of years together Vince, almost our whole lives, and I've watched you go though more than your share of hell. I think know you better than that."

I glanced back with a smile and headed toward the elevator. "You're a good friend George…, always have been. Don't know where I'd be without cha."

George shrugs and smiles back.

George, my lifelong friend, helped design the 'Star Shark' and acts as both pilot and sometimes body guard, and most importantly as company. We've been to hell and back, together, with the discoveries we've made and what our own people had put us though because of it all. And along with my children from a previously failed marriage on board with me, that was sufficient company. But lately, if George wasn't trying to play match maker for me then it was Maxx, the name I've given to the ship's computer, which has acted all too human since the discovery of the mineral polynesium, and its incorporation into his massive system. Indeed it has often shown almost human like qualities in the concern it seems to have for me, shockingly so. The holograms, created by Maxx, were his way of helping me to feel less alone while on my long voyages, even though solitude was precisely what I was looking for by coming out here in the first place. But I have often found myself responding to his all too real looking apparitions in spite of myself. My own self denial perhaps. Denial that I was a lot lonelier then I was willing to admit. Perhaps coming out here, was my way of, not only escaping the abuse and torment that I had received from my own fellow beings, but also to escape any chance of a relationship that just might turn bad again. There was no way I was going to bring that kind of pain on myself a second time, and yet here I am chasing down a strange and haunting dream. For what?

After a shower and a change of clothes I remained in my quarters for a while to reflect. Staring out the window at the vastness of empty space that lay ahead was something I often do, along with talking to myself. The dreams that George mentioned are haunting indeed, and I wish I knew why I kept having them night after night. It was not the same dream, but the same players acting out scene after scene of an endless play. The images seemed to come straight out of the History Channel with visions of a people living a life as they would have some hundreds of years ago, stone and wood houses, grass roofs, butter churns, out houses, the works, yet combined with styles and designs still unfound anywhere in our own Earth's history. Strange indeed. Maybe I was losing it after all, spending too much time alone out here in all this big empty nothingness. But it all seemed to be more than a dream, so vivid it was. It was as though I was living a second life every time I closed my eyes. But there was one face that always came back, one person in the dreams that I kept seeing over and over.

"Who are you?" I quietly asked the reoccurring image in my mind. "What am I seeing? What in the world is wrong with me? Maybe George was right."

"Bridge to Captain," chirped the intercom startling me back to reality.

I reached over and touched the Vidcom on the end table beside the couch. "Captain here, what is it?"

"Your mystery planet sir…dead ahead. And there's something else."

"Give us a two hundred mile standard. I'll be right there." I got up trying to shake the images from my head and made for the door when I suddenly stopped and chuckled. "So, lessee. I talk to myself, I'm talking to a dream that I had last night and the night before, and now I'm carrying on a conversation to with a holographic projection." I walked toward the door as it gave way to my movement. "Nope, nothin' wrong with me."

The doors to the bridge split as I push through. "Status."

The hologram sitting at helm control spoke first. "We're currently at 199.6 miles altitude standard circular, still cloaked, passive scan shows no readings sir, all clear."

"No readings on long range ether sir," the hologram at the navigation added. "All clear."

"Except…," the helm officer began again. "For an instant, as we settled into orbit, I could have sworn I had something. It was just for an instant…,then nothing."

"Play back the scan log," I commanded.

"Nothing on the log sir. It was too brief."

"Play back visual." The navigator pushed buttons as I leaned over to look. "Put it on the main viewer." The image on the big screen in front of us, that displayed the planet below, now changed to display the recorded image. "Whoa…back it up…there…now one frame at a time…HOLD!" The image showed the planet, stars, and a blurred shape in the distance. "That's it?"

"Yes sir," responded the navigation officer. "Not enough to really to get a good scan."

"Long ranged picked up nothing as we approached?" I asked again a little perplexed.

"Nothing."

"Well, there's either something there or there's not. Run a diagnostic on the main scanners for the fun of it." I stood staring for a moment. "An echo?"

"Sir?"

"Whaddya got planet side?" I asked, now directing my attention toward the science station.

"Nothing terribly exciting really," responded the officer pushing buttons on his control panel. "Earth like, with a variety of conditions based on location. Local inhabitants appear to be pre-industrial by several hundred years."

"Well, If our scanners did in fact pick up something out there," I began to speculate, "and if that WAS a ship we saw, it obviously didn't come from there."

"Except for this..." The science officer pointed to the screen in front of him that had an enlarged area of the planet showing. There was a small dark spot.

"What's that?" I asked leaning into it.

"A large void. A place where the scanners pick up absolutely nothing."

"That's impossible. Enlarge it." We both then stared in disbelief.

"It's approximately a quarter mile in diameter," said the officer reading off his display. "And, apparently, preventing any scan from penetrating to its source. And just a thought, It will also have a negative effect on communications. That is if you decide to use the T.D.S. to go down to have a look, and then have a need to come back."

"Impossible." I was becoming more confused than ever. "Unless..."

"Unless?"

"The only way to play that kind of trick on OUR scanners is to use our own technology against us, someone who has also discovered polynesium and is using it the same way we are. Otherwise it's impossible!"

The doors to the bridge snap open again allowing George entrance.

"I thought we were the only ones," The hologram at the science station asked. "Anyone else make such a discovery?"

"Well, not exactly."

"Our generous good captain here," quipped George throwing in his two cents, "while he was keeping our newly found secret away from the warmongers on Earth, decided to share it with our new found friends the Pasarin's."

"Well, they saved my life," I said, quickly defending my motivations. "OUR lives, actually. They were the first people we discovered, the very first inhabited planet we came to. We crash landed and they put me and my ship back together. I owed them...I trust em."

"But they refused it,"

"Yes, they refused it because they were frightened by it. They are not..., a war like people and were afraid of where this technology may lead them, as a people, I mean." The group looked closer at the small black spot on the science screen. "But...,"

"Yes...," George agreed as he peered over my shoulder.

"Maxx?" I headed for the door. "Scan the local inhabitance. I'll need some local clothing."

"Acknowledge."

"George, the bridge is yours."

"Whoa." He stopped me short. "You're goin' down? You're not going alone."

I paused for thought. "No, I suppose not." I reached for the vidcom. "Sam, will you come to the bridge, please."

"On my way," the Vidcom responded. I have no Idea why I insist on doing things alone sometimes. There's that wall again.

CHAPTER TWO

PARADISE FOUND

"Well, how do I look?" George and the kids were already gathered together in the T.D.S. room waiting for me. Dressed in our new attire, George and I had hopes in being less obtrusive in regards to the local populace, however, this attempt was about to be put to a test. "You're lookin' better than me," I said noticing the selection of clothing my companion had picked out for himself. Just then snickering and giggling broke out among my kids. "What?" The response was only more giggling. "Something wrong with the way I look?" The giggling intensified. "Don't answer that. You guys are silly."

Walking over to the large monitor on the wall, opposite the main controls for the T.D.S., I began to study the image it displayed of the planet below, just as it was on the bridge moments earlier. Touching the screen I moved the image about then spread my hands out wide causing the image to zoom into a selected location. "Ok Mel," I pointed. "Put us down right here."

"There's a long walk," George commented noticing the distance.

"I thought we'd hit that village there and see what we could learn first."

"Still a bit of a walk." He gave me a nudge. "Someone you hope to see there?"

"Once we make it inside this dark area," I said, ignoring him, "the ship will lose our tracers and we're on our own. It's acting like a massive E.M. pulse jamming everything from our scanners to our communicators.

"Because our communicators work off the same principal," my friend added.

"Exactly. Besides, I didn't want to be seen by the locals appearing out of nowhere. Looks like you could use the walk anyway, my friend." I patting George's stomach. "Obviously, something just ain't right down there. Whaddya say we find out what?"

"Well, I didn't get all dressed up for nuthin." George took a big breath. "I suppose I'm in for a little adventure. Let's do it. Strange to see you going down without your glasses though."

"Yes and these contacts are irritating my eyes. Let's go!" George and I stepped up onto a large, glowing, circular pad that thrummed under our feet. Immediately, an electrical charge could be felt tickling our skin as we found ourselves suddenly bathed in a powerful magnetic field.

"Locked and ready, Dad," Mel called out, making the final adjustments.

I looked over at George. "You got the gold plugs?"

"Yes I do," he responded.

"Scanner in the pouch?"

"Yes I do."

"Rock n' Roll. These weird shoes are hurting my feet already." I give Mel a nod, "Let's rock!"

As Mel worked the control board the vibration of the pad began to intensify and hum loudly. The tickle that inundated our skin intensified as well, and eventually grew into a full-fledged itch.

"Bye Dad!" Sandy piped at the last moment.

"Bye Dad!" Ian repeated. A quick bright flash and we were gone. The ship faded around us and was quickly replaced by a multitude of new color and shapes, merging forming our new surroundings. In an instant, we found ourselves enclosed about by a forest as bright sunshine worked its way through tall trees, a warm breeze gently patting us down. Birds could be heard in the thick wood all around as an otherwise bare grassy plane opened up before us just past the tree line, down a hill. The forest then continued on again just beyond a small village that lay about a mile ahead, nestled in the center of the plain.

"Ya know," George said rubbing and shaking himself all over, "I'm not sure I'll ever get used to that."

"There's really nothing to worry about," I reminded, "It's not like it's actually taking you apart or anything." Just then a powerful feeling began to build inside as I took in my new surroundings, distracting me. "It's a dimensional shift process…, that simply moves you…, from one place to another…, inter-dimensionally of course…,wow, beautiful. And so…familiar." A serious déjà vu began to envelope me as we started our long walk down the hill toward the village.

"Just thought of something," George piped still trying to rid himself of the itch, "What if the energy field expands enough and we find that we can't get back to the ship?"

"Because of the EM field?" I asked. "Are you saying that maybe we should have brought a shuttle instead?" My companion just looks at me with a bit of trepidation as a feeling of being marooned sneaks in and adds itself to the list possibilities. I push up my sleeve to reveal a watch hidden underneath and held it close. "Captain to Shark."

"Then again maybe it's already expanded and we're too late," muttered George.

"Faith my good man. Captain to Star Shark."

"Shark here Dad, go ahead." George and I give each other a look of relief. "Sam, scan the dead zone, and guide us in."

"Ah…It's approximately eleven degrees to your left and about five miles through," responded the watch.

George with the pocket scanner in hand points toward the distant forested hills. "There, just beyond that rise."

I raised my watch to my face again, "How's our tracers?"

"We still have a lock," said the watch, "but, there appears to be periodic interference. Nothing really to worry about at the moment. Wait…, hold on Dad…, The E.M field appears to be growing a bit."

"Growing?" George and I stop and look at each other.

"It appears to be much stronger then about an hour ago and covering a much wider area then when we first saw it."

"How long do you calculate until it reaches the village?"

"It's not growing that fast, I'll give it a day or so, maybe two."

"Keep me informed. Captain out."

"We're not heading back?" George hoped.

"No, we've got time," I said trying to sound confident. "I wanna head for that village first, and then we can sneak away and come back in the Cuda maybe." We continue our walk down the slope toward the small village. "Man this looks familiar. I've been here!"

"We've never been here."

"I know but…, I would swear I've seen this before, I know I have."

"Skipper?"

"Yes"

"Your fly is open and I can't stand it any longer."

"Huh?" I look down and found the fly to the big puffy pants open and quickly seal it closed.

"If I may ask, what was that sticking out?"

"Well," I laughed, "I have my regular clothes on underneath this weird get up and my shirt was sticking out." I thought for a minute. "How long was it like that?"

"Ever since you walked in the T.D.S. room."

"You're kiddin'! You mean it was like that the whole time?"

"Yip."

"And that's what everybody was laughing about?"

"Yip," George laughs.

"You guys are bad." I shook my head which got another laugh from George. A few minutes later we cleared the trees as the planet's afternoon sun gave a warm welcome to our expedition.

"You know, these shoes, or whatever you wanna call 'em, just don't swing it for long walks," I complained. "I don't see how the locals can stand 'em, and these contacts are irritating my eyes like crazy. I want my glasses back."

"Man, I'm gonna need to sit down and rest somewhere," George said adding his complaint to the list. "By the way, you got some sorta plan when it comes to tryin' to communicate with these here locals?"

"Not really. What happened to all that military boot camp training?"

"How long was that?" He chuckled.

"Not THAT long ago, you still should be in great shape, I would think," I said eyeing the growing bulge around his middle. "Is the scanner runnin'?"

"Yeah, but it's gonna take a while. First it's gonna need to hear the lingo, and even then it'll take a while 'cause there's no base to start from. It's, most likely, gonna be a whole new language system."

"Well, I guess we're just gonna have to play it by ear."

"Play it by ear, that's funny."

Eventually, we came up on some houses set on the out skirts of the village, made mostly of stone with wood frame and thatched or grass type roofs. The familiarity with my surroundings became strong.

"Wow, it's like I know this place!" I tried to soak in everything I see as we continued our hike. "Over on our right..., that house down the road there? An ol' lady lives there. And over there..., a mother with three daughters. They have goats, or whatever those things are, and...,"

"Three daughters," repeated George a little surly. "Goats. And just how could you possible know all of this? Wait..., don't tell me..., all of this was in your dream."

"Don't mock me George, I'm not making this up, and I know I'm not going crazy, so please don't mock me."

"Sorry Skipper, it's just that..., well..., you'll understand if all of this seems a little hard to swallow." Just at that moment an older looking woman came out from behind a shed and started working her way toward her house.

"No way," George demanded with instant denial. "Coincidence." I took a glance over to the house on our left as we past it but could find no one about. The ol' woman, however, stopped and stared as we walked past.

"Straight through town here," I began again, "then turning right into some sort of village square, a market place or other I think."

"I'm just following you, ol' buddy."

CHAPTER THREE

INTRODUCTION

As The dirt road led us into more a dense part of the village, I noticed that the buildings and houses were all made the same way, rock and stone with wood frame and were no higher than two stories as grass and thatch covered the roofs. The structures became more crowded together the closer we got to the center of the community. In spite of the trouble we took to dress and blend in, that "out of place" feeling started to grow inside us as the locals began to take notice of our arrival. The first thing I noticed, however, was the obvious lack of men from about age of early teen to old age.

"Ya know this is a wonderful little village here. It's beautiful, But something is amiss."

"Um…Skipper?" George gave me a nudge. We stopped walking for a moment for a glance around.

"You…, notice it too?" I asked. "Didn't Maxx get the local apparel down? Why are they staring? Just keep walking. Act normal."

"Act normal?" We resumed walking again. "What do I know from normal? Ain't never been here before. What's normal?"

"And something else," I added as I began to speak more quietly.

"What's that?"

"You see any men?"

Yeah, there…, there…," He pointed.

"Old guys, small kids, you see any young or even middle aged guys?"

George looked around. "Just those dudes on horseback."

"Yes, all wearing the same colorful garb. Uniforms I would guess and all armed with swords and some sort of small version of the crossbow. Where are the men?"

Eventually we found our way to what, indeed, appeared to be a market square in the center of town. Filled with what seemed to be large a collection of fruit, vegetables, clothing, pots, and some unrecognizable items. Women, both old and young filled the market square pouring over the wares.

"Well, what did I say?" I gloated.

"Every town has its shopping market," my companion insisted still in denial. We continued to walk around a bit, trying not to stick out too much which seemed to be rather impossible, as we now appeared to be drawing even more attention.

George was checking out some odd looking fruit, veggie, or whatever it was, when I touched him on the shoulder. As he laid it back in its display crate and turned to look, I made a gesture toward a group of women across the square.

"Rock n roll."

"What?"

"There," I pointed again discretely. "A mother and three daughters."

"Oh come now," George scans the group. "How can you tell who belongs to whom in that mass?" As we kept watching, one of the older women in the gathering walked over from one bunch of crates to a different set of crates containing what appeared to be bread and small fruit. Three younger ones followed. "Coincidence. It's got to be."

"Two in a row?" I gave my companion a glare. "What's it gonna take?"

"You gonna tell me there names next?" George taunted.

"You keep mocking me and I'm gonna put ya in the brig when we get back."

George chuckles. "Sorry."

"Actually there is one name that keeps coming back to me."

"Here we go."

"Molly."

George looks down and shakes his head, "Ok, you've gotta bet. If one of those is Molly I'll sit in the brig for a week."

"You're on." Slowly, I worked my way over to the ladies, who were still standing at the crates, coming up close enough to watch but keeping my distance.

"You're gonna make a fool outta yourself, ol' buddy," I heard George mutter quietly as he stood back at a safe distance.

I understood not a word of their language but it was certainly clear, what was coming down. The older of the women looked to be in mid seventy's. Her face and clothing told of the hard struggle that her life had been. She was chattering frantically to an old man seated behind his crates of goods, the proprietor obviously. The old man in turn was chattering back waving his arms at them as if to get them to finally leave. The three younger ones, looking to be somewhere between twenty five and thirty five years, their faces appeared to be yet unstained from the hardships that seemed to befall them. Well used and worn out aprons covered dresses that had obviously seen better days. The three just stood and looked on at the old man's exhibition with sad faces as the confrontation between the two continued. Eventually the old woman gave up and looked as if she were about to leave.

I gestured over to George to come over. "Gimmie your bag for a minute." I reached into the pouch still hanging around my friends neck and pulled out a few plugs. They were gold coins I had Maxx manufacture before we came down. Gold anything seemed to be accepted pretty much anywhere we went and carrying some around certainly seemed like a good idea, especially when it came to food and lodging. "George, would you say that most of these people are dirt poor and starving? Let's see what we can for these."

I walked over to where the ladies were standing and was observed immediately. Without attempting to speak, I held up one coin for the old man behind the crates to see, and then tossed it to him.

He caught it, and with shock and amazement looked it over. Biting down on it and checking it again, with eyes as big as apple pies, he glanced back at me. I said nothing, but gestured to the goods in front of him and then to the ladies. The old man then took the baskets the ladies were holding and one by one began to fill them. We were communicating.

"You're good deed for the day," George commented with a smile. Then out came a large, very full, cloth sack. Flour perhaps? Two of the younger ladies began their struggle with it when I took over and picked it up for them. They all began to chatter and giggle amongst themselves in obvious joy over the chance of events that befell them that day. As far as the old proprietor, he started to show off his new prize being sure he got the better end of the deal. The older lady came up to me with tears in her eye and began to chatter and bow.

I took her by the hand and kissed it sporting a big smile. "I'm sorry, I don't speak your language, but you're very welcome." Little doubt they understood my language as well as I understood theirs, but I was sure that the feelings that were exchanged that day were quite sufficient.

The four of them stood looking at each other rather perplexed for the moment but then slowly, they began to walk away looking back as if to say, "Are you coming?" I stayed right behind following them out of the small square with their large and very heavy sack. The smile on their faces, to me, said it all. Their arms were as full as my heart.

"George", I whispered to him, "Have you noticed how gloomy these people are? When I watched 'em smile just now it was as though they've never smiled in their life."

"Suppression perhaps," George conjectured.

"How so?"

"Well, look at the guards or whatever they are, stocking these people. I mean, they certainly look like guards, roaming around on their horses like this is a prison or something."

"Yeah. I wonder. Ya know, they don't exactly fit in, do they? Almost like there're not from here."

"You mean like when the English took over Ireland?" George's comparison turned on a light.

"Or…, maybe another theory I'm thinkin' about," I added.

After a brief walk to a horse and cart that stood waiting, we placed the merchandise within, and watched the younger women push themselves up and sit in the back with their groceries. The older woman climbed up in the front and picked up the rains to the one horse that will pull them all. They then sat and turned to face George and I as we stood there watching them back. After a short and awkward moment of chattering amongst themselves, they held out their hands and waved us over.

"Rock n' Roll, I think we're being invited to dinner," I walking over to the cart as George followed.

"Awesome, I'm starved."

Of course, George and I were more than happy to take a ride with three of the most beautiful ladies in the village, so we pushed ourselves up next to them and took a seat. Mama jerked on the rains, made a noise, and with a small jolt, off we went. George and I were definitely all smiles, as the young ladies in back with us began to giggle now and then. I'm sure they must've had a ton of questions; what's your name, where are you from, with what language you're speaking, etc. But with that kind of barrier standing between us, we had to be satisfied with smiles and giggles, at least for the moment.

Breaking the awkward silence I spoke first. "Sisters?"

"Most likely," said George sporting smile on his face.

"How old do they look?"

George chuckles. "Old enough. The blond one's been eye ballin' you like crazy. Strange look on her face too." As I looked over at her she quickly averted her gaze.

"Well, I can't speak for her but it's like I've seen her somewhere before, all of 'em actually."

"Hey," George shrugs, "I'm hooked. I'm just gonna sit back and see how this whole thing plays out now."

Remembered the three plugs that remained in my pocket, from what I took out of George's pouch, I thought of a way to break the ice. I put a big smile on my face and looked around. The two brunets eagerly smiled back with a giggle. The blond, however, appeared to be preoccupied. When our eyes met she looked down again, blushing. The one brunet to my right then said something to the other brunet which made them both giggle. The blond, failing to see the humor in what was said, took a swipe with her hand at the first brunet, which caused the two to laugh even louder.

A Perfect moment. I reached into my pocket discreetly and put the plugs in one hand. With the other hand I took one of the plugs, hid it, and held up my seemingly empty hand for all to see. All went quiet. I even had George's attention now. Ever so slowly I took my seemingly empty hand and moved it over to the blonde's face.

Her look changed. I'm sure she thought that now might be a good time to take a dive off the cart out of fear, if not for shear embarrassment.

With a smile still fix on my face I slowly reached behind her hair toward her ear. She froze. I then changed my look to one of surprise as I pulled my hand back again now holding one gold coin.

All gave a burst, causing George to jump. The blonde put one hand to her ear stunned as I put the coin in her other hand. Giggling and chattering erupted as George shook his head chuckling.

"I'm sure they need other stuff...," I told George. "... dresses, food...,"

"Sure. I get it."

Right about there any ice that had remained melted away, at least for the brunets. Mama then turned to see what the noise was all about as the blond showed off her new prize. It was now Mama's turn to squeak.

Now it was another's turn. The brunet to my right. The cart went dead silent as I took her hand in mine and waved my own open hand over hers and then closed her hand tight. I then sat back and waited. She looked at me and then opened her hand. Another burst, more giggles, and chattering. Another gold coin.

"Ok now that was good. How'd ya do that?" George asked looking a little closer.

"Oh just a trick I learned from somewhere."

"One more," he nods toward the remaining sister. I reached out to the last one and took both of her hands and placed them together in front of her. "A la peanut butter sandwiches," I chanted as George laughs. I sat back. She opened her hands to reveal my last coin.

"Ok, I'm sitting right next to her and I didn't even see how you did that one," he said perplexed.

George and I sat back for a while watching the girls enjoy their new coins, knowing that each of which could buy many new dresses, with shoes to match and, most likey, a horse or two to go with it.

I tapped myself on the chest, getting their attention again. "Vince." I then touched George. "George." I then point to the brunet sitting next to me and waited. The cart went silent for a bit, as the girls looked at each other and chattered, except for the blonde whose mouth seemed to drop open. I did it again, "Vince…, George." And then pointed to one of them. The message got through as the brunet next to me spoke first.

"Marrigiglinela."

I made an attempt at it. "Marig…la…ooh."

She laughed and spoke a bit slower, "Marr-igig-line-la."

"Marig…la…line…Mercy." Abandoning it I looked to another girl.

"Kerrilinagitala."

"Oh man…," I chuckled.

"You walked right into that one buddy," George laughed. I decided, right then, that shorting their names would be a matter of self defense.

"Mary and Kerry," I said pointing to one then the other. Both girls broke out in giggles.

"Mary, Kerry, and…," I stopped and waited for a response from the blonde.

In an almost inaudible whisper she finally spoke, "Molligilintalna."

"Molly," I whispered in a bit of shock, as pieces started to come together in my mind. "Molly." The whole thing now seemed harder for even me to believe. We held each other's gaze as she now started to looked a little frightened.

"Skipper." Breaking my concentration George pointed down the road where we had been. The men on horseback were now headed our way.

"Following us?" I asked. "You suppose we drew more attention then we should have?"

"We'll see."

"Keep yer eye sharp." I then pointed to where we were headed. "George, look." It was the exact house to where I said these ladies, whom I said did in fact exist, did in fact live.

"I take it all back," George said finally caving in. "Really I do. I don't know what to say. This whole thing totally blows me away."

"I hope you find the brig nice and comfy," I said reminding him as he laughed again nervously.

Mama took the horse and cart past a two story rock and wood house to a barn looking structure that lay in back and to the right of the house. Scheming quickly in my mind, I made sure to jump off before the girls did, or should I say, before Molly did. I quickly made my way round the cart and held my arms out to help her down as the she began to jump off. Rather silly of me I know, but somehow I felt I compelled to do so. Another awkward moment ensued in my attempt to be chivalrous causing her to stop, but then she proceeded again very slowly. I took her by the hands, which trembled, and helped her down, our eyes fixed as uncertainty still remained in her face. She said something quietly to me and then left for the house rather quickly.

"You're welcome...I think," I said as I watched her go. George said nothing as he watched, but simply busied himself helping the ladies with the goods to the house.

As I stepped into the house I felt extremely humbled. Very little furniture decorated the home as a very old table stood almost center, pitted and scarred from what seemed to be centuries of use, some chairs, most likely from the same century as the table, wrapped around it, and similar chairs in what seemed to be the living area with a few drawings or painting on the walls. These people needed more than just a few coins. I suddenly felt embarrassed at my so called generosity.

Mama quickly made herself busy around a huge fireplace that seemed to come equipped with everything she needed to cook with, right off of the wood that was burning inside it. The large flame was the only light in the place aside from a large oil lamp that sat in the middle of the table.

"Wow," George whispered.

"Wow is right, humbling to the extreme. George, I need you to find your way to the outhouse or somewhere private and check the E.M. field to see how far it's progressed, if at all."

"Gottcha."

"Check in with the Shark too. It's getting rather dark outside so be careful."

"So far this has been an awesome trip, I'm sure glad I came along."

"It has," I whispered back, "it really has."

As George found his way back outside, I found a chair and relaxed and began to watch the shadows dance on the walls created by the open hearth. The floor creaked heavily anytime somebody moved about adding to the atmosphere that seemed to encircle us.

As simple as it was, it really felt like home. The house was warm, and the popping and crackling of the fireplace could easily put me to sleep. I felt like I could find peace here, a kind of happiness that I never knew back on Earth. Earth, yes. How spoiled we are. Or even me with my automation and replication and instant gratification. Of course I also knew that the reality was, that I would find this life a whole lot of hard work even to survive day by day, being used to my automation and instant gratification as I was.

I looked up from my thoughts and caught Molly studying me. I wish I knew what she was thinking. What was that sudden fear all about?

As I glanced up, she had been pulling something out of a bag that lay on the floor, two metal rings the size of jar lids, and looked as though she was about to hold them up. As she caught my eye she began to slowly put them back in the bag. What was she doing? She quickly turned her gaze as if to be busy. Sometimes that second quick glance is so irresistible however and as she did so, I gave her a big smile. A faint smile came back to me as she turned her glance once again to her task. Whatever it was about me that made her afraid I hoped that it would eventually abate.

As I watched the ladies busy themselves with the dinner preparations, one of my favorite songs came to my mind. I must have played it or hummed it a thousand times before now, and it totally fit the moment I was witnessing. I began to hum, a smile still dressing my face. Mama glanced over an approving smile.

Once again I had Molly's gaze. This time She was giving a look of curiosity. Did she recognize the song? She walked over slowly, rings in her hand again, and sat in the chair next to me, continuing her study as if trying to look deep into my thoughts for an answer to some mysterious question. I continued to hum. Slowly she brought the rings up and held them close to my face.

"Hello Molly," I whispered to her. She froze for a second then dropped the rings on the floor making a clatter that broke the calm in the room, rose up with eyes as big as the dinner plates and ran up a flight of stairs. I was unaware that George had come back.

"What happened?" He asked.

"I'm not completely sure. It's like she saw a ghost."

George took the empty chair next to me. "According to Sam, the E.M. field is now two miles in diameter but appears to be holding for the moment. Although, he did say the frequency and the pulse spectrum that make up the field are three times the strength they were."

I breathed out slowly putting the pieces together. "George if my theory is right…this whole valley is in danger."

"You're not thinkin' that maybe…,"

"The Pasarin's…are the only ones aware of the existence of not only polynesium, " I continued, "but the technology that goes with it. Why do you think they wanted us to stay away from here?"

"Somebody may be trying to put together one of our reactors, I figure," he conjectured.

"But why turn us down, just to sneak off and build your own? That just don't make sense. Why not just ask us for help from the start? Ya know, polynesium is nasty stuff. If that's what they're doing, and if they're getting it wrong…"

"You get a nasty pile of hot goo."

"Well, without a proper governor controlling the reaction you're more likely gonna get a…,"

"A very big boom-boom?" he finished again.

"You get a runaway reactor that will eventually atomize," I corrected him. "And if they're, by chance, sitting on a cash deposit of even more polynesium, still buried underground, the resulting explosion will take the entire valley out…, or more!"

"Mmmm, happy thoughts. And that's if, in fact, there is more of the stuff here. We really don't know that."

"True. That's a long shot to say the very least, but what else would attract 'em here? Someone somewhere must've found something."

George rubbed the back of his head. "Well, here's one more happy thought for ya. The ship's scanners did indeed pick up another ship in orbit. Evidently, they've been having trouble maintaining a cloak and the Shark finally picked it up."

"And?"

"Pasarin."

"No Surprise. I think these nice folks are gonna put us up for the night, so when they do we'll sneak back to the Shark and take a closer look at our friends in orbit, and possibly even rattle their cage a little."

CHAPTER FOUR

TAKEN

The dinner conversation was rather lax, due to the obvious difference in lingo not to mention a little awkwardness that hovered about the table, but I have never had a better meal in my life. I'm not sure what it was on my plate, but I sat back quite full and amazed at what these ladies could do with so little.

After thanking them the best I could and giving Mama, as I call her, a big hug and a kiss, Mary lead us to the barn for the night. There, blankets and straw would keep us warm, that, with the one horse and a collection goats that came and went out the other side of the divider would keep us company. George, right away, tried to make the best of the straw and blankets, as I remained in the open door, the cool night air patting my face, with something strange in the open field, nearby, making its usual night noises.

A dark silhouette stood motionless at the upstairs window as the light of their moon gently lit the field that surrounded the house and barn. I stood looking up, watching her stand there with a collection of feelings stirring around inside me. Somehow I'm going to reach her, one way or the other. And, of course, it may require me to do a lot more than just learn their language to do it. But why? What in the world am I so anxious for? I don't even know the girl, not to mention the planet I'm on. What am I thinking? The first cute blonde that comes along and I think I know her? Maybe George was right. I blew her a kiss and waved anyway just to get a reaction. She left the window. But then, unexpectedly, she came back to the window and waved. "Well, whaddya know." I went into the barn, closed the door and laid down on my blanket. "One giant leap for mankind."

"What?" George asks, finally laying flat on his blanket.

"Molly waved at me just now."

"Wow! Truly." We lay in silence listening to the animals on the other side of the wall and the strange critters out in the field.

"My feet are killing me."

Suddenly, Yelling and screaming startled George and I causing us to bolt up and dash toward the door. "WAIT!" George opened the door a crack and peeked through as the screaming and yelling continued.

"They're hurting them!" I cried, trying to push past him.

"Wait! They're coming!" He closed the door.

"Stand there!" I commanded pointing. We each took our place on either side of the barn door, so as to be just out of sight as they came in. Looking around, I spotted a pitch fork laying in the straw in the far corner, strange looking, but a pitch fork none the less. I picked it up and took my place by the door again. "I'm really not looking to kill any of 'em, but…,"

"I understand," George whispered. "I don't suppose there's time to have the ship just pull us out?"

"I'm not gonna just up and leave the girls!"

The door burst open as a man with gold chest armor and sword at the ready stood in the door way looking around. Spotting George he began to raise his sword for a swing as

I came out from behind the door and rammed the handle end of the pitch fork in his ribs just under the chest armor. As he doubled over, I then came up with a blow to his face knocking his helmet off as he fell to the ground.

"You're getting much better at that, ol' buddy," whispered George.

At that exact moment an arrow blew past me and buried itself in the far wall. Ducking back behind the door with George stepping further back into the dark on the other side, another soldier stepped in behind the first. Again I used the pitch fork, in the ribs, and up to the face, and down he went. We stood there for a moment waiting for others to follow, as the yelling and screaming continued to split the night air, but no one else came.

I took a step out of the barn and glanced around outside. "The rest must be looking around in the house and out the field for us."

"I saw six," said George behind me.

"Well then…, two down, four to go."

George gave me bad look.

"I thought you said you didn't mind a little adventure."

"Not this much!" He quipped dryly.

With my heart now beating wildly, I decided to make a mad dash toward the house with pitch fork in hand, stopping suddenly, eye balling the swords that now lay on the ground in front of me. Throwing George my pitch fork, startling him, I reached down and grabbed up a sword, turning it around checking out the blade. "Alrighty then. Let's do this."

Spotting my movement, a soldier standing near the front of the house began his own run toward me.

"Head down!" George shouted as he gave the pitch fork a heave over me. Sailing over my head, the pitch fork met the soldier half way, finding its mark in the soldier's right foot pinning it to the ground.

"Nice shot, George!"

At that instant another soldier bolted out of the house, sword in hand. Through the open door I could make out all four ladies huddled together sobbing.

The soldier and I faced off, slowly, circling around, waiting for the other to make the first move. Or so I thought. Turns out my opponent had another game play.

The sudden warning from George came all too late. "VINCE!!" With a heavy blow, exploding on the back of my head, the world around me went black.

*   *   *   *   *   *

The floor felt cold and damp as I slowly regained consciousness. Waking up in the dark is a little disconcerting as one tries to put ones perspective back in focus. And it doesn't help if one can't even see what that perspective is. My head throbbed horribly and the smell in the room was nearly as painful.

"Oh man, my head…oooh." I Sat up and looked around. Except for what little light came through a very small window located too high on the wall to reach, the room was dark. A nasty looking cot could barely be seen laying along on one wall and a big metal door prevented any chance of escape. I pushed up my sleeve. No watch. "Oh wow." I rubbed the back of my head as I stood up. "oooh."

"You speak the tongue of the king!"

I jumped out of my skin grabbing my chest. "Good night man! Don't do that!" Did he just speak English? I moved over closer to the mysterious voice trying to get a focus on him in the dark. Tongue of the king? Who in THIS world would speak English, or even Pasarin for that matter? Although some Pasarin's did learn English due to my lengthy stay a few years ago. "You seem to speak it pretty well yourself. Who are you?"

"Personal slave of the king's chamber, Manotu." The voice in the dark sounded old. The hair and beard, of what I could see, gave a clue to either this man's time in prison or his service to his king, or both.

I went over to the big metal door. "So why are you here? You get caught trying on the kings whitie tighties?" Jerking on a door that you know is locked is rather impulsive. It tried it anyway. It's locked.

"Speaking in the king's tongue is…death."

"And I suppose you learned it by spending a great deal of time around the king?" I asked.

"I was heard speaking the king's tongue to the other servants and was sent here."

"Death…" I pondered that as I as I sat down beside the old man still rubbing the back of my head. "Just suppose you tell me about this…king." Whew, this boy's smells like he's been here awhile indeed.

"It is death to speak it!!" He got up and began to pace nervously, yelling frantically in his native tongue.

"Tell me!" I insisted. "…please." His pacing continued around the small room as he continued to unravel before me. I grabbed him and shook him. "It's the only tongue I have, I speak no other!" Looking at me a little shocked, he then slowly sat back down. "Speak and I will free you." He watched me intently as he slowly gathered back his senses, then continued.

"It is said that he came from the sky. You speak his tongue. Do you, also, come from the sky?"

"Go on, please, tell me about the king."

"It is also said that he seeks power from Maru."

"Who is Maru?"

"Do you also seek power from Maru?"

"Manotu, who is Maru?"

"You must not seek power from Maru! You will not find it! You will kill us just like the king!" He was beginning to slip away from me again.

"Manotu, I do not seek to kill anybody! Who is Maru!"

The old man then appeared to grab what little sanity he had left and began again. "Maru is here, everywhere. Maru is the land and the sea. The power of Maru puts the grain in the fields, the fruit on the trees!

I sat back adding a few more pieces to the puzzle. Of course. Maru is the planet, or at least that would be the logical conclusion. The Pasarin council would have never revealed this little fact, or the fact that they may have found a cash load the stuff right here on this planet. All they wanted was to have us stay away from here. But, why not tell us, or ask for our help to begin with? And if this, so called, king is from Pasaris, why then is he using English instead of using his own Pasarin language? They, or someone is seeking the power of Maru for themselves…the power of polynesium. "Manotu, how long has the king been here, when did he arrive?"

"He came down from the sky five harvests ago." Fear still seemed to be churning away inside the old man.

"Did he find the polynesium, I mean, this power of Maru? How much has he found? This is very important!"

"He came down from the sky and took us for slaves and sent us down in the caves. Five harvests we spent digging and clawing looking for the power of Maru. We found nothing. Maru hid it from him. The king's anger grew and there have been many deaths because of his anger. Many women are now without husbands, children without fathers. Many go hungry because of his desire for power. All now live in fear!"

Odd. If they haven't found it, then why would they think it's here?

"SKIPPER!" A voice echoed from somewhere outside the little room. "VINCE!"

"You must not seek this power!" Manotu began slip into his tirade once again.

"We do not seek it," I said attempting to reassure him. "We have come to free you and your people."

"We have?!?" yelled the voice from outside the room.

I get up and push my face in the bars in the small opening the door. "George? That you?"

"Yeah man! Where you been? You ok?"

"Pounding headache but, ok I guess. How long was I out?"

"We've been here for a few hours I think, hard to tell. Thought maybe they hauled ya off somewhere or killed ya or somethin'. What's this stuff about freeing the people?"

"I've got a roommate, found out a few things. You should hear what he has to say about what's goin' on around here."

"He speaks English?!"

"So it would seem."

"You just can't seem to stay out of trouble, can ya ol' buddy. So…how do you plan on doing this heroic deed from inside a dungeon cell, or whatever?"

"I don't suppose you still have your watch?" I asked.

"No, they took everything; watch, scanner, coins, everything. Communicators won't work anyway. Tried it on the trip here, before they swiped it. This castle or whatever this is, appears to be the center of the dead zone we saw. So what's the plan?"

"I'm still wearing my regular clothes underneath this other garb."

"Yeah, and…,"

"I'm wearing my belt."

George was ecstatic. "They didn't take yer belt? So what are ya waiting for?"

"I was gathering some intel."

"Gee, you finished? Let's get outta here!"

"Manotu, it's time to leave."

"What are you going to do?" Manotu asked still wrapped in alarm.

I stepped back from the door and smiled. "Use the power of Maru." I reached inside my outer clothes where my belt was hidden. The buckle had a quick release and was immediately loose in my hand. "Stand back please." Manotu slowly stepped back and took position against the far wall. I held up my buckle and aimed carefully for the lock in the door that held us prisoner.

CHAPTER FIVE

ESCAPE

I fully expected to have the usual bright flash with the usual loud bang, which would then be followed by the usual smoke coming out of the now blackened door, and so forth. But as I pressed the small button on the buckle, FIZZZT. A few sparks came out then nothing.

"Oops…hmmm." I looked the buckle over.

"What's goin' on?" hollered George, becoming impatient.

"The E.M. field around here must be messin' with it." I could hear George's head hit the metal door that was keeping him confined. "Wait…" I touched a couple of buttons and aimed again. "Let's try a higher setting."

"Yes, lets," George growled with a note of sarcasm.

Suddenly a bright flash exploded out from the buckle hitting the large, heavy, metal door causing a thunderous bang that echoed down every corridor. The door slowly swung inward as smoke poured out of a large burned hole where the lock used to be. Being totally over come now with horror, Manotu, buried himself in the back wall and began ranting in his own tongue.

"Wow man!" George shouted. "That lit up the whole corridor! Gimme outta here before somebody comes to find out the heck that was."

Running out into the hallway and looking for George's door, I aimed my buckle for a second volley. "Stand back, way back." BANG! Another deafening explosion filled the corridor as the heavy, metal door slams inward against the wall. "High is the only setting that seems to work it would seem."

"I'd love to see what that would do to a guard," George said as he quickly joined me in the corridor.

"Manotu, come, this way. Manotu, let's go!" Nothing but silence came. "Manotu!" I looked back into the small room. Manotu became a permanent fixture on the back wall with eyes as big as the water bucket on the floor. He appeared to be quite content where he was.

"I think he crapped his pants with that one ol' buddy," joked George, as he began to take off down the corridor first.

"Poor guy doesn't know what to make outta any of this. Scared him to death. Actually, I'm not totally sure he was any wearing pants."

We jogged down the maze of corridors, past a series of locked cells as one or two had strange sounds emanating from inside them, but most were silent. Up ahead around the corner footsteps could be heard echoing throughout the network of passageways.

"Quick, down here." We ducked quickly down a dark side corridor and waited. Two overly dressed guards quickly passed us heading down the main passageway where we had just been.

"Any second they're gonna notice the open cell doors," I whispered, "Not to mention the smoke."

"I think those colossal bangs were a dead giveaway, don't you?"

"Time to get outta Dodge." Resuming our race down the corridor we saw another side passage, only this one had an open window at the end.

"An open window?" I thought. "That's kinda crazy." Racing to the window we looked down and were met with a surprise. "Wait a minute! Somehow I got the impression I that this was the dungeon!"

"Whatever, as long as it's a way out, know what I'm saying?" George eye balled the drop. "We're a...two maybe three stories up! Well...the good news is, there's water to catch our fall." Sometimes George's humor just doesn't brighten the moment, but this time he just may have the right idea, and at the moment it may be the only idea. Down the hallway footsteps were heard once again. Both of us looked out the window again trying to make a very quick decision.

"Sure hope it's deep, cause if it ain't we're dead."

"What?!? Your kiddin', right?" My quick decision seemed to be just a little too quick for my partner. "I was only joking! You're crazy!"

"You have another idea? I'm open." It didn't take long for our guard friends to find us at the window. The language they were using was not my own but it was certainly clear what they were saying.

"Is this where I start repenting?" George asked. Pulling out their crossbows the guards dashed for the window after us. One at a time we stepped out onto a ledge, pushing off into the open air, diving feet first toward the mote below. Although George has often claimed to come along as my body guard and protector, he seemed to be the only one making noise as we fell.

SPLOOOOSH!! The water, thankfully, was indeed deep. Hitting hard, we went down several feet before managing to fight our way back to the surface gasping for a breath of air again. Moving quickly, we swam our way to the edge of the mote and climbed up the embankment on the far side peeking around to what lay beyond.

"That seemed more like five stories. Don't ever make me do that again!" George panted. "Not as long as we both live!"

"Hey marine, I thought you were a pilot, no jumping outta planes, no parachuting?"

"I prefer to land in the same perfectly good aircraft that I went up in, thank you!"

"Mr. Adventure," I laughed. Looking around at our new surroundings we found an open field, horses in a coral, and a road that runs to a forest that lay just beyond. "Think we can make it to those horses?"

"Well, it's not too terribly far but, far enough."

"Yes...," I said agreeing with him. "Far enough to wind up with an arrow up our backside." Once again we began to hear the tell tale yelling of guards as one sounded the alarm to all the others. "The time is now I think." We climbed out cautiously. "Be quick and stay low." My soaking wet clothing made me feel heavy as I moved. It seemed like forever as we worked our way across the field in broad daylight to the coral of horses. "George, it just occurred to me. No saddles. Can we do this bare back?"

"Right there." George pointed to three horses just outside the fence complete with saddle and bridle.

"Rock n' Roll," I said rather surprised "So..., where's the owners, out takin' a pee somewhere or what?"

"Never look a gift horse. And before you ask," George blurted, "Yes, I do ride. I just don't jump out of airplanes...or ten story windows!"

"It was three, and you never told me you never used a parachute before," I said following after him, over to our waiting rides. "How'd you ever avoid it?"

Just at that moment several guards on horseback came thundering our way on their own horses along with a couple of arrows that sped past our heads.

"GO GO GO!!" I shouted. Each scrabbled over to the horses, jumped on and began to ride off, in different directions.

"No Skipper, this way!"

I immediately turned my horse around and followed my companion. We had a good head start on our pursuers but their rides seemed to be faster, after all, they were the experts. Me, what do I know about riding, I only command a starship.

Into the forest we went, turning and twisting along an endless winding road that seemed to head to nowhere. I did my best to stay right behind George but began to have my doubts about our direction. "You sure you know where you're goin'?" I shouted.

"This is the way we came," he hollered back. "Trust me! I was the one that was awake, remember?" Our rides continued to pound down the dirt road as the dust filled the air behind us.

"Ya know I really don't have a lot of padding on my backside for this!"

Suddenly, two guards on horseback appeared in front of us, each lowering a lance blocking the road the instant we were about to pass. Amazingly George managed to duck and ride through in spite of their plains to the contrary, but the lances caught me in the chest hard knocking me off my ride. WHOMMMP!

With the wind knocked out of me royal, and some new pain to my back and legs, all I could do was to lay there and wait for the inevitable. "Oh...man! Where in the world did they come from?" George stopped quickly a few feet past the guards who had just traded their lances for crossbows, both of which were aimed at me.

I reached in for my buckle and clicked it loose. Too many of them for me to start shooting, I'd catch an arrow for sure, but I had another Idea. As the guards jumped off their mounts, crossbows at the ready, I threw the buckle in the air in George's direction.

"George!" I yelled. "It's got a transponder! Get out of the zone, Maxx will find you!" He caught it! "GO, GO!" I yelled again.

But he hesitated, not wanting to just leave me. "I'll be back, this time with some disrupters!" By this time the guards, that were giving chase, had dismounted and joined the others in aiming their crossbows.

"GET OUTTA HERE! GO!" George took off. Several arrows whipped past over my head missing George by mere inches. One of the guards remained on his horse and gave chase leaping over me and past the collection of crossbows. I hurt too bad to move and so I decided to just lay on the ground motionless. I let out a big sigh. "Go George go…, please let him make it."

*　　*　　*　　*　　*　　*

Once more, I found myself thrown back into a small dark room as the guards shackled both my hands to the wall this time and then left, bolting the door behind them.

"Make sure I can't move, ok?" I hollered back to my captors as they left. "Make sure I can't even reach down to scratch my…," another sigh, "butt."

It would seem somebody definitely wants me alive. Otherwise I would have been either sent to the mines with the rest of the male population, if that's where they are, or killed on the spot. But why? Why am I so important that they want me so badly? Wow am I hungry, and a might thirsty.

"Hello!" My voice seemed to echo through the room and down the empty corridors. "Manotu?" Nothing but dead silence came back. I was alone.

My out stretched arms, chained to the wall were already proving to be wearing. My clothes had been taken away from me to remove any possibility that I might have more hidden gadgets still on my person somewhere and instead, they had given me a pair of over sized, puffy, very thin, light brown pants, that seemed to be made out of some sort of silk. So in other words, not only would I starve or die of thirst, but now I also had the option of freezing to death.

Jerking on chains, you know couldn't possibly give, seemed rather impulsive if not a little impetuous. I held still for a moment and listened to the dark that surrounded me. The light in the window was gone as well as night had come to those in the outside world. Ever so faintly, outside my little dark room in the corridor, I thought I could hear what sounded like moaning. No, crying. Yes, It was crying. Maybe it was a woman or even a small child, but to what cause would anyone have to imprison either one. I listened carefully to it as the sound seemed to come and go.

There was no way to tell just how long I hung there. After what seemed ages, light had eventually made its way back through the small window again high on the wall. Morning had arrived.

I hurt. My arms and back were killing me being held in the out stretch position for so long, especially after the hard landing I took being knocked off the horse which only added to the tenderness. I'm so hungry and so thirsty. Sleep had been absolutely impossible and I am so very exhausted.

I listened again to the emptiness to see if I could hear the crying that I heard last night. It seemed to have abated for the moment. All was silent. I closed my eyes and tried to focus on something that might take my mind off this, for at least a moment if I could. Something that would lift my spirits up and out of this room.

Molly. Thinking about her, if nothing else, had always brought me some comfort. For years when I slept on board the ship I felt as though I was slipping into a completely different life. Images of someone named Molly as well as others, in a life very different than the one I had been living, would quite literally take over every aspect of my being. Not a nightmare in the least but instead something quite unexplainable. And this planet I was on…, is this the world I was seeing? And Molly and her family, were they the ones that came to my mind as I slept? Was she the same Molly as was in my dreams? Was that possible? How could two people be so linked, so connected, and yet, over such a great distance?

Just then, as my eyes remained closed, images, sounds, smells, and feelings of fear and horror came rushing to my head.

"Wow," I whispered, in a bit of a shock. I tried it again. Closing my eyes again I concentrated. The images came, as I began to see a big metal door, a room, dark, small unfold in my mind. Feelings also flooded back to me as I then felt cold, frightened, confused, and felt like I was crying.

"This is silly," I cried out loud. "This whole thing is making me go crazy! Bloody room is pulling my mind apart."

Talking. I hear talking now. I listened. It was very faint. Sounds like the same voice that was doing the crying. Young boys can often sound like women. Hard to tell. Can't tell what's being said though, sounds like the Maru'in language. Naturally, ya moron what else would it be? I closed my eyes once again and began to concentrate. This time the image that I saw was of the large metal door closer up as though I was looking out the small window in it, pushing my face in the bars. Could it be? Could it possibly be? Most likely I finally loosing it. Too many long lonely nights spent by myself talking to my computer, just as George had said. With a sudden wild notion I yelled out as loud as I could, "MOLLY!" I expected nothing, as it was only a shot in the dark as it were, but I listened. The talking stopped and there was silence for a moment. I closed my eyes and focus on her and then repeated my own name in my mind over and over.

A very weak and delicate voice came back from somewhere in the dark beyond the door, "Ence."

Horror struck me as I opened my eyes wide! They have Molly! They do! They have Molly locked up! Why would they do that! One more way to get at me perhaps? To what end?

I was about to shout out again but was stopped by the sound of footsteps echoing down the maze of corridors. Stopping outside my door, it was followed with the sound of metal clanking and rattling until the door to my room swung open. It my good friends the guards.

"The men's room is down the hall to yer left," I piped. The guards said nothing but came over with a four foot long dowel which they proceeded to shovel into an open loop in my left hand shackle and pushed it through until it reached the other open loop in the right shackle. "What's with the broom stick?" Still as silent as ever they then unlocked my shackles from the wall, as the dowel kept my arms in the out stretched position keep me from doing anything except being very cooperative.

Once I was freed from the wall, a large hand gave me a shoved with such force it caused me to hit doorway with my out stretched hands almost knocking me on my back. The stick, which made me too wide for the doorway, had to be turned sideways to get through. As soon as I'm free I know exactly how I am going to vent all of this pent up anger.

Bracing for the next hard shove I made sure I turned semi sideways down the hall to keep from hitting anything as I walked. Sure enough, the next shove came. I grit my teeth. Your turn will come my friend. Your turn will come.

As we proceeded down the corridor, our footsteps resonating throughout the maze that lay around us. I believed I could hear the crying again, as it appeared to be getting louder the more I walked down the hall. One of these cells that lay ahead perhaps. I kept walking until the sound appeared to come from behind the door that we were just passing,then I paused.

"Molly!" I hollered quickly. A dirty, tear streaked face came to the small bared window in the door.

In a weak voice Molly responded again, "Ence." Right then the anger within me raged. The guard behind me shoved again, this time hard enough to cause me to hit the floor face first. I somehow managed to find my feet again, even with with my arms still locked in the out stretch position, and turned to face him. I stood at him nose to nose, for a moment, with my teeth clinched and all the fire in my eyes that I could muster. The smile he had been sporting seemed to fad a bit. Yes, the prisoner, indeed, might do something crazy. I turned and continued to down the hall, this time without giving the guard the satisfaction of another push.

CHAPTER SIX

THE WOLF

Upstairs, down hallways, up more stairs. We finally arrived at two big wooden doors which one of the guards pushed open and then proceeded to shove me inside.

It was a large room. The decor was fit for a king indeed. The stone walls had fine wood frames with inlayed carvings complete with gold touches as red velvet drapery hung on the oversized windows. Two of the walls had swords on display while a small table against one wall had what looked to be our two watches and a pocket scanner, or at least what was left of it. An attempt was made to disassemble it which apparently activated its self destruct mechanism. I would have loved to have been there to witness that little moment. The remaining wall had a huge hearth with a roaring fire that was proving to be oh so welcome.

In the center of the room was a large table with fair set for what could have been enough for a whole company. The first thing that came into my mind when I saw this incredible bounty was all the empty tables that I witnessed out in the village.

With the exception of myself and a guard standing on each side of me the room stood empty as we waited there. But we didn't wait long as in through another door came a heavy looking man who obviously spend most of his spare time in front of a plate with fork. He was wearing a red silk robe with a purple sash, and had black shoulder length hair penned back in a pony tail complete with a closely sculpted beard. Wasting no time finding his place at the table, He got right to work filling his plate.

"Captain, you must be famished." His voice was as thunder. But what startled me more was his perfect English and the fact that he seemed to know who I am. His face did, however, begin to look familiar to me.

"You seem to have me at a disadvantage."

"Oh come now Captain, Nilsson is it? I know for a fact that you're smarter than that." He looked up briefly from his feast. "I'm sure you've got it all figured out by now." He held up a sizeable chunk of meat on a fork. "I have to tell you, the cooks on this planet are excellent. You must try some of this roast monkle. They may be several hundred years behind you and I, Captain, but they could sure teach a thing or two about the culinary arts." His eating habits certainly lacked the grace of any royalty, but his tactics were indeed working, and quite well indeed. I was absolutely starved and all this food being waved in front of my face wasn't helping matters at all.

"When I left…," I said trying to get my bearings, "Pasaris was a peace loving world. Sense when did the council start engaging in conquests other planets, especially ones like this?

"Very good Captain!" A-Meel responded. "You are an intelligent man, but conquest? You see me as your Cortez conquering the new found world do you? The council is nothing but a bunch of soft hearted, weak minded, sheep, who failed to recognize an opportunity when they saw it! An opportunity you provided, I might add!" I seemed to have gotten under his skin right off the bat. "The council refused your offer if you recall, Captain. All of them accept one." I was now beginning to get the picture.

"Yes…," I suddenly recognizing him. "A-Meel Me-lot."

"I'm flattered Captain! You do remember me!"

"Well, you do look a little different."

He chuckled, "As I said," he patted his stomach, "they've been real good to me here.

"To bad the same can't be said of you," I mocked, throwing barb. "You know what you should do is dye your hair white and maybe get yourself a set of reindeer, you could make post cards for the holidays."

"I do not know what that means, my friend," he said, still stuffing your face. "But I would like to take you up on your offer. If fact, I think we could work together in building that 'new world' that we all talked about."

"You and me?" I laughed. "After your very warm welcome I was definitely thinking the same thing. You kidnap my friend and I, strip me down, lock me up, shackle me to a wall, my wrists are bleeding, and now you're talking to me as though nothing happened, like we're old buddies, like we're still in your council room on Pasaris? Your people are at least one hundred years ahead of my world. Are you afraid of me, Mr. Me-lot?"

Suddenly my captor wasn't appearing quite so relaxed as he was a second ago. "I think we have a lot we could offer each other my friend, you and I. We have, as you said, an opportunity of a life time here, right now."

"You're not answering my question."

A-Meel paused his meal and started to glare.

"If I recall," I said starting another volley, "your plans included building weapons, bombs and a change to a socialistic order, more guns more control, more…"

"It needs to happen!" He interrupted pounding the table. "Our world is falling apart, Captain! Chaos is everywhere! There needs to be a change and a stronger government to make those changes if we are to survive as a people. Even now my world has enemies that could…"

"To survive as a people?? Explain to me how destroying this civilization makes it right. Explain to me how stealing from these people and raping their land then, putting them to death helps your world." The pole holding my arms straight out appeared to be loose in its loops. If I could just slip one loop out it would free both my arms. Keep him riled up, I thought, keep him distracted. Although, if the guards notice what I was doing with my hands I was dead. I continued to needle him. "The chaos, A-Meel, is you! This is why you were removed from the council in the first place. That's why they took your seat from you. You were caught creating disruptions throughout the governing city on Pasaris, and all over in fact, in an attempt to rally the people to your favor! And now you're completely destroying an innocent and beautiful world here." Now, I could see his anger raging in his face. Just another inch or two with this pole is all I need.

He came from around the table. "You know nothing of our world and absolutely nothing of this one!" He pounded the table again. His face was as red as his robe now. "Like the council you are blind! Totally blind! Our world is too weak to stand up to any threat that may come upon it and it needs to be made stronger, much stronger, and you gave us that power my friend, you did!"

I soften my voice, "You mean like the threat that's happening to these innocent people here." There was a silence. I could see his eyes ready to burst out at me at any moment.

"Let's…,as you say, cut to the chase, shall we Captain?" He said brisling. "You have the technology that I need and I aim to have it." A-Meel was trying to keep himself under control, the same failing control he was using on his home built reactor.

"Yes, I did notice you were having a wee bit of trouble."

"No doubt that became obvious when you entered orbit," he said softening his voice in an attempt to recompose himself. "I need your help. I need the technology. That's all I ask."

"And if I don't help you out, you'll wind up blowing yourself and this castle to fragments, all the way back to Pasaris. Frankly, I don't see the problem."

"The problem is…, Captain," he growled, moving his face to close to mine. "Your little girl friend from the village is down stairs locked up. Yes, we noticed your little doings with some of the locals, all warm and cozy. One I noticed in particular. And there she will stay. You see, I'm no longer asking. I am going to get your help with this reactor one way or the other."

CHAPTER SEVEN

On The Loose

The blood in my veins was now boiling! And for the moment I had forgotten all about how tired I really was. "Why drag her into this?! What has she ever done to you? Or ANY of these people, for that matter? How many have you murdered, A-Meel? How many? How many in the mines, or those trying to escape from this hell you've created? What about their families, their wives and children that are now going hungry as a result of all this you've created, what about them?" My left arm was now freed. And although I kept my arms in their out stretched position, it was a now simple matter of swinging my right arm around and pulling it out of the loop of the right hand shackle. My heart was pounding.

"It's very simple, Captain. We you could put an end to it right now if you like." He walked back around to his food again. "To me they're just savages! Always will be. Useless. "

"They're a people!" I raged! "A people like you or me! Living beings…"

"They are not!" He interrupted. "They are not the same! Have you not figured out just who these people are? They are not like you and me! They are different!"

"Different how? They get up in the morning, wash, eat food, crap in the outhouse, then go home and write stories about it. How are so they different?"

"Captain, these people…, their way of life…, it's thousands of cycles old! Maybe hundreds of thousands of cycles!"

"And…?"

"Don't you see? They're just not capable of any development what so ever! They just can't! And there's something else strange about them too." This whole conversation was now exasperating me beyond words. In the corner of my eye I noticed that the guards had gone glassy eyed, having to stand there and listen to the bantering that A-Meel and I were doing, in a different language, and not understanding a word of it. And with A-Meel fully distracted and seething, the time was perfect.

"Have you ever thought that maybe they like it that way? That don't make 'em savages! That perhaps some sort of religious belief plays a part in this? Heck man, I've only been here a very short while and found more peace and happiness in their way life then I ever have on my own world!" A-Meel's eye's seemed to light up as he leaped from around the table again.

"Well then, Captain, the solution seems simple enough! Let me have the technology I want, and you live with these…, people…, in peace! I'll spare them all!"

"Ah, gee…, let me think about that," I mocked. "Hmmm…, No, my fat, greedy friend, I have a slightly different idea." With the pole firmly gripped in my right hand, I swung it around to my left freeing it out of the right loop and landing it squarely in the face of the guard to my left. Without missing a beat I swung it back to the right nailing the other guard on my right. Swing it left again I hit the same in the back of the head and then around for a second hit for the left guard. Both went down.

By this time A-Meel had bounded over to the wall, where his prized swords were hanging and grabbed one. The guards here always carried their half sized crossbows hanging off their belts cocked and at the ready. I quickly dropped to the floor and grabbed the nearest one and aimed it at A-Meel who had come within a few feet of me. We both stood motionless.

"If you think you're faster with that sword then I am with this trigger...," I warned. Time seemed to stop for a moment as I waited for A-Meel to make a very important decision. Eventually his sword drooped in his hand. "All the way to the floor, thank you. And back up against that wall over there," The sword hit the floor. He stepped back. I picked up the pole that held me captive and put it in the door hooks so no other guards could inter the room, at least not through there anyway. Then, being very careful to keep my eye on my fat friend, I found the keys and few spare arrows that hung on the guard and proceeded to remove the shackles from my wrists. I then grabbed the other guard's crossbow. My wrists were bleeding, my arms killing me, along with my bruised and hurting shoulders and back, but for the moment I had ignored it all. With two crossbows now aimed at my wide target, I moved slowly toward the other door.

Anger now seethed through A-Meel's gritted teeth. "You have just sentenced these people to death, Captain. Their blood is on you!" I opened the other door and began to step through, keeping my eye on my captor.

"Oh and one more thing." I held one of the crossbows a little higher, aiming it carefully. "This is for Molly." Pulling the trigger release, an arrow streaked across the room finding its mark into A-Meels's left thigh causing him to hit the floor in a scream of pain.

After reloading, I quickly made my way down hallways and corridors, then down stairway after stairway. I fully expected to find a lot more guards about, but maybe they're spread pretty thin which served to convince me more of a theory of mine as to where the guards actually came from. Although only a theory, this still may prove to be useful later.

Peering around a corner with crossbows in hand, I noticed only one guard around, or at least he's the only one that I could see at the moment. He appeared to be fascinated with something or someone inside one of the cells, making comments in his native tongue then laughing. Crying could be heard coming from inside the cell. That was Molly!

I walked cautiously toward him, but he seemed to be too hung up on his personal entertainment to notice my approach. And as if taunting her through the door wasn't enough he then reached down unbolted the door and swung it open.

I raised one of the bows and fired as the arrow then sailed through the air burying itself in the of the neck of the tormenter. He jolted and fell to the floor grabbing his neck choking and gagging, as a short scream came from inside the cell.

Throwing the one empty crossbow to the floor I ran to the open doorway and found Molly in her own state of shock with hands to her mouth standing there frozen.

"Molly!" She didn't move. I ran in and touched her on the shoulder. "Molly!"

Looking up she reached out and grabbed me. She stood only five foot four and very petite. Her eyes were full of tears, her face dirty and streaked. The top of her dress was ripped as she held it up to keep herself covered. It would definitely break anyone's heart to see her. If this was the guard that did this to her, he's certainly paying for it now.

Reaching down to the now lifeless body I removed the jacket. "Yer done with this aren't ya buddy?" I Held it open in front of Molly who then stretched her arms out as I pulled the jacket over her.

No time for chit-chat. Taking Molly by the hand I raced down the corridor looking for that one familiar passage way with the open window in which George and I used; at least I hoped it was still available.

Found it! But just as we turned the corner to make out way down to the window, I could hear more voices and footsteps coming down from the other way. I pressed my back against the wall and waited for them with crossbow ready. Molly joined me as though she could sense what I was doing.

The guards walked passed not noticing us, that is until I got their attention.

"Psssst."

The guards stopped and turned, noticing the crossbow aimed in their face they froze.

Just then Molly spoke. "Yeete nota maneete!" The guards dropped their own weapons on the floor as I looked at Molly with surprise.

"Wow," I cried out loud. She ether had a forethought to my plans or is reading my mind. "You go girl!"

Motioning the guards to walk on down the hall, Molly picked up the weapons and proceeded to throw them out the window.

"That'll work," I approved. Finding an empty cell, I opened the door and motioned the guards in then bolted it behind them. "Let's go before we get any more visitors." Taking Molly by the hand again, we ran for the open window once more.

I looked down toward the mote below and gave a sigh. "Not again. I thought I'd only have do this jump only once." Yet again Molly's sixth sense was on alert.

"Neea," she squealed looking at me, shaking her head.

"Come on, it's only…," I looked down again, "three stories." Even if she did understand me I don't think that would have helped, cause it certainly wasn't helping me. The guards that I had pinned up were making such a huge racket that I was certain we were going to get more unwanted guest at any moment. I stepped up on the window's edge. And sure enough, right on cue, more footsteps, running this time. "We haven't got time to debate it, lady! Come on!" As our new arrivals came around the corner I jumped. "Ok legs straight, feet first." Wow, what a rush. SPLOOOOSH!!!!

Once I Fought my way to the surface I took a huge breath of air. As frightening as that was I actually found it strangely exhilarating. I looked around. No Molly. Looking up, I found that she still remained frozen on the ledge of the window, screaming. Obviously trying to decide which was the more frightening, the guards or the jump.

"MOLLY! JUMP!" I hollered. "COME ON, JUMP!" I was so afraid I would have to work my way back into the castle to rescue her once more. She kept looking down at the mote far below and then back into the passage at her captors, screaming.

Then finally, she jumped. As she fell the rush of wind pushed her dress up around her face. Oops! I averted my gaze. No bloomers! SPLOOOSH!! She disappeared underneath the water.

A short moment later Molly's head popped up as she swam to the mote's edge joining me, still wearing the ripped up dress with a backwards jacket, breathing hard. She said nothing, but still looked as pitiful as ever. I swam over to her still holding on to the rocks, took her by the forehead and kissed it.

Without waiting for a response I climbed the embankment and peeked out at the grounds beyond. The sun would be setting soon which may give us some cover later, but there was plenty light out now. Wait a minute! Where's my crossbow? I must've lost it when I hit the water.

While I was thus planning our escape, I suddenly heard some odd sounds coming from behind me. Rip, rip, rip, rip, tear, and rip. Then rustling. I was afraid to turn and look. After a short moment Molly then climbed up and peered over the embankment with me. I looked at her. She apparently had removed the jacket, tore away the top of her dress until only the skirt remained, then put the jacket back on the right way around.

"Comfy?" I asked. I continued scanning the ground beyond. No handy horses, all saddled up and waiting as before. I wonder if there's time to get to the coral over there, let a horse out and ride away bare back, and do it all while staying alive. There was no doubt in my mind that Molly could ride, saddle or no, but was there time.

Out from nowhere a guard approached on horseback from the left. We ducked down. Did he see us? We held still and pressed ourselves against the embankment. Just then Molly had another idea. She worked her way over to my right side then climbed up out of the mote standing in plain view of the oncoming rider! I was shocked!

"Molly! What are you doing?" I hollered. Has she gone crazy? As the horseman approached her she walked backwards a few more feet, thus putting my position directly behind the horse. As the guard stopped in front of her, I began to see her plan.

"Clever girl." I could only guess at their conversation but, at that moment I was more concerned with timing. Being as quiet as I could I climbed up out of the water and came up behind horse and rider as it was now or never, being that the rider had just begun to swing his leg around to dismount. With one hand gripping his jacket I jerked him down from the horse, then grabbing his head with my other hand I pulled it down as hard as I could as my knee then came up to meet his face. As soon as I made the saddle available, Molly climbed up and waited for me. I grabbed the guard's crossbow and pulled myself up behind her. She then gave the horse her heals. So far we seemed to be making a good team.

"Yic, yic, yic!" The beast took off like a shuttle launch as the cold wind seemed to blast straight through us, reminding us of how wet we were. We weren't alone either. Others noticing our escape took off in our direction as the arrows wiping past our heads gave warning. If we could just get past the coral and into the forest just beyond we may be able to lose them.

As I turned to look behind us, one guard managed to get ahead start past the pack of riders that followed not far behind. Closing in fast he raised his crossbow. Our horse had two riders while his only one; the odds never seemed to be in our favor at any time, but I still had no desire to go back to that cell again, or whatever A-Meel had planned next. Gripping my crossbow tight I did my best to aim in spite of the horse's hard gallop. But just at that moment, an arrow cut its way toward me finding its mark. Crying out my left hip began to burn with excruciating pain causing me to almost fall off the horse right there.

"ENCE!" Molly yelled, hearing my cry and turning to look. I reached back for the arrow but instead of finding it, I pulled back a bloody hand as Molly screamed again. Gritting my teeth to hold back the pain, I attempted to re aiming my crossbow back at our pursuer who was all too close now. I fired. The arrow sped back toward the guard burying itself in his face, knocking him off his horse.

I could feel the blood down my running down my hip now. The pain was unbearable. I don't feel so good. I think I'm going to…, pass out.

CHAPTER EIGHT

BONDING

I kept my head down low doing my best to hang on to as much reality I could, but with my lack of sleep, food, and now the loss of blood it was all finally catching up to me. As we road on I seemed to fade in and out, and eventually I lost track of where I was altogether.

Suddenly I jolted awake, we had stopped. Molly jumped off our ride causing me to almost fall off, losing her support as she dismounted. After helping me down, she gave the horse a smack on the backside and sent it on its way rider less down the main road. One would only assume that she had managed to lose our pursuers somewhere as we rode into the darkening forest, at least that was my hope. I was most certainly going to be more than a burden to her now, in any case. Standing up on my own was impossible now. It was as though every ounce of my energy had poured itself onto the ground back there.

Taking my arm and putting it around her neck, Molly then lead me off the road and down a steep hill hidden inside a thicket of trees deep in the forest. "If this is what it takes to get you to put your arms around me", I told her drowsily, "I should get shot more often." After some walking we soon found another path and began to traverse it for awhile, going deeper and deeper in the forest. I was definitely going into shock, as I now seemed to be freezing and shaking uncontrollably.

Waking up again, discovering I had passed out once more, I found myself on my back rolled up in a dirty worn out blanket in a shallow cave of sorts. Molly must have somehow carried me the rest of the way down and over to this spot. I tried to envision a five foot four, petite woman dragging a five foot ten, one hundred seventy pound man. But then I envisioned her carrying who knows how many buckets of water around, laundry, moving a plow, chopping wood, dragging it in from the forest, carrying it in the house, and anything else she and her family had to do on a daily basis, all with no man around. Yeah, I guess she could do it.

I still had the shakes and was very cold as I laid there bundled up the best I could get out of these blankets. I figured I had lost more than a bit of blood on the way and was still in shock. Pulling the blankets up around me tighter I looked around. There were other blankets, pottery, utensils of sorts and other things all lining the cave on one side. Others had been here. Perhaps those people who were escaping the castle came here to hide out or to rest up before taking up the trip again, like a safe house of sorts.

As I tried to sit up, I was instantly met with a stabbing pain over my left hip. Looking down at myself I found some cloth wrapped around my middle. And over my left hip, in back, the cloth was pressing some sort of plant, that had been ground up, against the wound. Herbs of sorts' maybe. My pants were still damp from swimming in the mote and now soaked with blood as well. And now so was the blanket I was laying in.

The entrance to the cave was wide and partially over grown with weeds. In the late evening sun I could hear birds, the wind, and a river that must me a short distance from the cave.

Just then Molly came in with a bowl in her hand. She was stirring something in it as she knelt down beside me. Her skirt seemed a wee bit shorter now, and tattered. Now I know where that cloth around my middle came from.

"Dozha," she said, as she held the bowl up to my face. Trying to sit up I winced in pain and lay back down, it was too excruciating. Quickly, she got up and fetched another blanket to put behind my head and back.

I tried the bowl again. It's warm, how'd she get it warm? Starting a fire would certainly have signaled our whereabouts. Looking in the bowl I found some mashed up leaves or roots or whatever it was in warm water. It tasted surprisingly good as I took some in. After a few sips more, I laid back against the pillow blanket, so exhausted.

Molly put the bowl to my face again, "Dozha noyea." Arguing with a woman on any planet, I found, was never a smart thing, so I took the bowl and downed the rest of the concoction.

"That's not too bad," I commented, as she took the bowl from me. As she began to stand up I took her arm I tried a smile. "Thank you," Giving me a smile of her own, she walked away with the bowl and went outside. It would appear this lady knows her herbs and plants.

I made an effort to get comfortable, figuring I'd be here for some time before I could gain enough strength even to stand up. I had lost a lot of blood through that wound, and that alone should lay me up for a few days. But just then it struck me that this may not be the greatest idea. Staying put would give A-Meel and his guards all the time they needed to find us. We may have to get moving soon, although right now I couldn't scrape up the energy even to crawl.

Molly came back with another bowl full of that same concoction along with more of some kind of plant or herb pieces she was holding in her skirt. This was causing her to show a bit more leg than usual.

"You are so beautiful," I told her. I wished that somehow she could understand me. "Smart and beautiful."

"Dozha noyea," she told me again putting the second bowl up to my face. I knew what that meant now, so I took the bowl from her, and this time downed the whole thing at once.

Putting the bowl aside she carefully rolled me over onto my right side exposing both blood soaked pants wound. After digging out all the old bloody plant pieces being held into place by the cloth, she then carefully washed the wound, and placed the old herbs with new. Rolling me back she checked the cloth strip for tightness then pulled the blanket back over me.

I could definitely sense more coming from her then just simple kindness as she tended me. In fact, I seem to be able to pick up on her emotions and thoughts in ways that I should not be able to. Was she able to do the same? As evidenced by the experience we shared while we were being held in the castle, there was no doubt that we were connected in some way, emotionally, mentally. How was this happening? What sort of magic was taking place here? As time went on, both of us will be found acting on this connection more and more, whether she was aware of it or willing to admit it or not. But the ultimate question still remained; how and why were she and I connected? How was this happening?

After she covered me completely again with the blanket, she moved over to my feet, reached in the blankets and fished around. I felt her take hold my pant legs and give a solid yank pulling my pants away completely. In all my years, this is the first time I have ever been pantsed, not to mention being pantsed by such a beautiful woman. I had no doubt she was just doing a job that she had done a thousand times before as washing and cleaning was part of her daily routine and thought nothing of it. I said nothing, what could I say, but simply watched her walk out with my dirty, blood soaked trousers. Even so, I did find the whole thing rather exhilarating.

After some moments she came back with my pant showing them to be a mite cleaner. Keeping my wound clean was vitally important but, blood stains don't always come out of clothing. But still, I was grateful for the effort, especially if all you have is a river to wash in. Instead of giving them back to me she hung them up on a rock at the entrance where the sun could dry them. Looks like I'm going to be stuck here in my blanket for a while.

Molly came back with yet another bowl, this time it had whole leaves and something that looked like wild berries and the like, only without the water. "yehne noyea." I ate everything she offered me then laid back. It was a good feeling to be full again. The shakes were gone and I felt very sleepy. Whether it was the herbs, the exhaustion, or maybe a combination of the two, I couldn't tell, I simply fell asleep.

"Wow what a dream." I sat up, wide awake and feeling a whole lot better. It was dark and raining lightly outside the cave. Molly had obviously gone to bed some time ago. I really shouldn't be feeling this good this soon. Whatever was in those herbs she gave me is certainly working, and nothing on Earth could do anything like that.

"What a dream," I repeated. "And what a sexy dream too. I wonder what brought that on." I used to dream about Molly on board ship but it was more like looking through her eyes at her daily doings, nothing like this. This time both us of were in the dream together. I wondered…,now that she and I are in close proximity I wonder if…" I turned to look at her. She was lying there rolled up in a blanket of her own, her eyes peeking out as big as can be, staring at me. She didn't move. "Oh dear." I sunk back down into my bed and peeked over at her again. Her eyes just glared. "Look, it was only a dream," I told her, "Can't control what I dream. Besides who says it was my dream, maybe it was your dream." She didn't move but her eyes said it all. "Yes ma'am." I shrank back into the blankets, turned over and tried to go to sleep, fearing what I would dream next. Oh my.

*   *   *   *   *   *

A warm breeze blowing into the cave accompanied by singing birds woke me from another deep sleep as the morning sun was doing its best to work itself into the cave. I don't recall any more shocking dreams again that night, just the usual collection of nonsensical images. Although I do recall Molly popping in now and again among the dreamscapes that presented themselves.

I turned over and I looked at her. She looked so peaceful still sleeping there all rolled up in her blanket, so beautiful. With this strange connection we've had, I feel like I've known her for some time. But there are still blank spots or unknowns that had to be solved. Still things about her that I had to discover.

Waking up in the morning has always brought with it the same natural physical rhythms, no matter where I was sleeping, and this morning was no exception. My bladder was full.

She appears to be sleeping rather soundly, and I can't wait any longer, so I made an attempt to go do something about my current emergency. My pants were hijacked last night for cleaning so Mr. Blanket will definitely have to come with me. Moving ever so quietly, while trying to keep the blanket wrapped around me, I made an attempt at standing up, which I found to be rather difficult.

"Whoa." Still a might dizzy. I felt good while lying down, but now that I'm standing on my feet I feel so weak and light headed. Even so, this is a far cry from what I thought I was going to be doing; that is laying around for days. I walked slowly out of the cave and into the morning sun. "Oh that feels so good." Sunlight bathed my skin, warming me as I made my way a good distance from the cave entrance.

As I responded to my bladder's distress call I could hear the river just some yards away, the birds in the trees which surrounded us on every side, and the warm morning breeze patting me down. I was definitely feeling better.

With the mission accomplished, my blanket and I made our way back to the cave. While I was trying to keep quiet, and not fall on my face, my blanket slipped from my weakened hands and on to the ground. Picking it up again I laid back down and snuggled in. Nope, I was not in any condition to run any marathons just yet.

I turned on my right side to look at my roommate again. Molly's eyes were wide open with a big smile on her face. Busted.

"Sena ottun," she said giggling.

The best thing to do when faced with an embarrassment, I found, is to pretend nothing happened, shrug it off, and then maybe change the subject.

"Hello," I said to her. At first Molly said nothing back, just kept watching me and smiling. I reached out and pointed to her month then to mine. "Hello," I said again slower.

"Hel…lo," she repeated.

Awesome, I've got her talking. "Good morning."

Molly responded in kind, "Good...morn...ing." The accent was heavy but otherwise perfect English. At this pace it would take forever to learn each other's language, but then again, what else was there to do.

Eventually Molly got up, straightened her skirt and jacket, made some sort of effort with her hair and headed for the cave entrance. After picking up two bowls she grabbed my pants and threw it at me, burying my face.

"Thank you," I responded through the pants.

A half hour later we were both sitting in the morning sun eating our breakfast of leaves, berries, nuts, and other things that she had collected that morning. I wasn't about to lay in that blanket for one more minute.

I watched her as we ate, keeping a smile on my face as she glanced over now and again. I was, without a doubt, taken by her. But what did I know of her? Our ways of life were so vastly different one couldn't even begin to count. And we have yet to speak each other's language. But the connection we shared could not be argued. We were definitely stuck together in a way no one would have guessed, not even ourselves.

There we both sat, tired, dirty, haven't bathed in a few days, ragged clothes, and our hair, quite the sight to see. But to me she was the most beautiful thing I've ever seen.

"Molly," I said. "Beautiful." She looked at me with a smile accompanied with a bit of confusion on her face. I repeated it. "Beautiful." She knitted her brow a little. I reached over to a flower that was growing just within reach, plucked it, and held it up. "Flower." I grabbed another one, this time of a different color. "Flower." I held them together close to my face. "Beautiful...flower." I could see her wheels turning. I then took my hand and put it gently on her cheek. "Molly...

flower." Her face went flush as she put on that 'shy little girl' look with a smile. I then gave her the flowers.

I decided to make an attempt at walking around a bit. Putting my hand on Molly's shoulder I made on effort to stand up, hopefully without falling down, as Molly put her hands out to steady me. As I stood up I kissed her on her forehead. I was hoping that she would pick up on the feelings I was sending as well as the words I was trying to teaching her. But there were plenty of signals coming from her as well, and as for my part, I was hoping to be able decipher them as they came.

As I stood there in front of her she reached around and loosened the cloth wrapping that still hung around my middle and let it fall to the ground along with the herbs it was holding. She then checked the wound as I turned and took a look at it myself. It had sealed itself! It looked as though it was almost healed over! This normally would have taken fifteen, twenty, maybe thirty stitches! Amazing! Just then something totally unexpected came out of Molly's mouth.

"Rock n roll."

I stood stunned as I gave her a look of surprise. "What did you say?" That was something I have always said now and again, but have never said it to her at anytime, how could she know it? I repeated it back to her. "Rock n roll."

Molly smiled. "Rock n roll."

I laughed as I squatted back down in front of her kissing her on the forehead again. It was so good to hear some solid evidence come right out of her mouth. I kept both of my hands on her cheeks and looked straight into her eyes. So blue, so beautiful, they seemed to be looking straight into my soul, as I reflected back on the past few years and that special connection we've been sharing, so close we've been and yet literally worlds apart. What in the world was happening? We studied each other for a moment as I couldn't seem to let go of her. I was getting very strong emotions from her now; very warm feelings yet she still seemed a little afraid. I could read it as though they were my own thoughts. I moved closer to her face and could hear her breathing getting deeper as I got closer. I can feel her breath on my face now as I was sure my heart was going to beat itself clear out of my chest.

CHAPTER NINE

ON THE RUN

Suddenly I froze. Out in the distance I heard a dog bark. No, two, maybe more. Seems my fear about hiding out here was now a reality. I was afraid that the blood I had lost was like an open invitation to our secret little hide out. The cave, being kept secret for some time and helping many to freedom, was now exposed. A-Meel had sent dogs to hunt us down and I had lead them here.

I jumped up. "DOGS!" Molly saw the fear forming in my eyes and gave a look of confusion. "Molly, Dogs." I put a hand to my ear and went quiet. Molly listened with me. We both heard them, and they weren't very far off now. As fear and panic gripped her, I quickly grabbed her arm as she jumped up and began to head toward the main path that leads away from the cave and into the thick forest. "No Molly, neea, neea, this way!" Quickly, I lead her down toward the river. "The dogs will lose our scent this way." Down to the river, and in we went. I just hope its deep enough for what I had planned.

"Wow, is this water warm or what?" The river was indeed very warm, almost hot! So that's where Molly got her hot water. We worked our way toward the middle of the river and found we were indeed able to submerge ourselves completely if we had to. Is it just me or am I having trouble staying dry during this whole trip? Then it struck me, this is how A-Meel is keeping his make-shift reactor from blowing its top! He's diverted the river to run through the castle in an attempt to use the water to keep it cool. Just how long will that work? An explosion still seemed eminent to me, the real question is; when? I may be forced to offer my knowledge after all, if not to save his hide alone, but the rest of the valley's.

Just then the dogs came down the path toward the cave accompanied by the guards. Molly and I both took a deep breath and ducked down in the water. As we did so I did what I could to help Molly coral all that hair and skirt in keeping it below the water line. How long could we hold our breath? We were about to find out.

Holding onto her under the water, I tucked Molly's hair inside her jacket then looked up toward the surface. I could see the guards walking around our camp through the ripples. Molly's arms tightened around me as a dog or two came up for a drink from the river. Each took a couple of licks then changed their minds. Too hot for a decent drink I figure. It was beginning to be too hot for me to sit in!

Then I remembered George and I's watches! The watches I stole back from A-Meel, they were still on my wrist, how could I have forgotten? As I held onto Molly I looked at both watches that I had strapped to my left wrist. Both were giving a 'no signal' reading on the display. We were still well within the dead zone being created by A-Meel's reactor, and I figured that it may be awhile before that changed, especially on foot.

Oh man, I hope they leave soon, it was getting harder to hold my breath. A few bubbles escaped from Molly's mouth. From below the water, I could still see the guards walking around, the dogs sniffing around. The scent ends here, I thought to myself, now go, GO! Oh mercy, my lungs are beginning to burn. More bubbles escaped from Molly. It looked like she was going to lose it before I would. I pressed my mouth to hers and gave her some of my air. Oh…please, my lungs, so hard now! Keeping my mouth to Molly's I hoped to keep her from breathing out too much then sucking in water.

I looked up through the ripples, seeing no one I put my head up out of the water ever so slowly. Were they were gone? Looking around I saw no one. Helping Molly pull her head up out of the water we both breathed in the awesome fresh air. Oh wow, I think that was the longest I've ever done that!

Looking around the camp to make sure the guards and their dogs had indeed left, I then looked at Molly, "You ok?" She seemed none the worse for wear, both of us were breathing hard and paused in the water for a moment to catch our breath. Brushing the wet hair out of Molly's face I looked to see if she was alright, then put my arms around her. "I'm so sorry. So sorry you had to go through this." Pulling myself out of the water first I put my hand down to help Molly out. We climbed out onto the bank on the other side where a large clearing in the trees lay, leaving our little cave behind on the far side. The clearing, we were now headed to, seemed to go on for a half mile then narrowed and was blanketed in short grass and wild flowers.

After walking a few steps I looked at Molly and saw tears forming in her eyes as she then began to cry. My heart sank, as I tried to imagine how hard it must be for her. A simple people, living a simple life suddenly put through such hell, not knowing or even fully understanding what was happening to them or what it was all about. I stopped and sat down beside her on a fallen tree, not knowing what to say or do to comfort her, but simply put my arms around her to give her what solace I could.

"Yeana noee eena," she began to say through her tears. "Ohno aseea." She went on to chatter, tears running down her wet face. I then remembered the event in my cell, at the castle, and closed my eyes to focus on her. After a moment I could see her home, Mama, and the girls Mary, and Kerry. Molly turned and watched me do it.

I opened my eyes and look at her. "Mama?" I asked her, "Mary, Kerry?"

"Eea," she responded nodding, as we both did our best to try and communicate. She was missing them. And this whole traumatic experience, being kidnapped, locked up, chased, and who knows what they did to her while she was in the cell before I came along. I stared at the ground feeling so terrible and so depressed.

"This is entirely my fault," I told her. "I caused this whole thing. If I had never brought that blasted polynesium to the council on Pasaris, in the first place, this never would have happened. A-Meel would have never come here to begin with and enslaved everybody and did was he did." Molly watched me for a moment, then closed her eyes like she seen me do. I continued on. "Just like on Earth, the same thing I was afraid would happen on Earth and I caused it here. What an idiot I've been. What a total and complete idiot…,"

Molly interrupted me by grabbing my face and turning it toward hers. "Neea, Ence, Neea…a…A-Meel…" She seemed desperate to say something. "Maru…A-Meel…" She was struggling. "aneu kara eena mona sateea…" She threw her hands in her lap in frustration. The language barrier that stood between us seemed to be winning out. I put my forehead on hers as we both closed our eyes, then focused. I wanted to see what this thing we shared could really do. I emptied my mind, focused on her, then waited.

What happened next was indescribable. Not words, but feelings came to my mind. After a moment I believed I could understand the basis of what she was trying to tell me. She feels that it was not my fault. She was blaming A-Meel for what was happening to her village and not me. However I did wonder if she truly understood my part in this whole mess; that much was still unclear, but what I could sense from her was very warm and passionate. I no longer sensed any fear aimed at me at all.

I opened my eyes and looked straight into her gorgeous blues then nodded, believing I understood. "Molly is beautiful," I said tenderly. She put her arms around me with her head on my shoulder and cried. I just sat there and held her.

CHAPTER TEN

CLOSE CALL

As our journey continued through the forest I tried to soak in everything I could see and feel. I took in the air, the trees, the flowers, it was so beautiful here. The sun warmed us, as well as our wet clothes, while Molly lead us through the large clearing in the trees. White flowers, looking very much like oversized daisies carpeted the ground around us. Checking the compass on my watch it seemed we were taking a longer way around back to the village, if in fact that's where we were headed. Although I really had no way of knowing just where we were, we were definitely off the main road, as was the obvious and safest plan. I guess I simply had to trust Molly in knowing where she was taking us.

Our walk became a very quiet one after almost being caught and nearly drowning in the river, and Molly needed some cheering up. She had been pulling up the daisies as we walked along so I thought I would give it some sound effects, just to see what she would do. As she pulled one up I made a sound; "putttttth". She pulled another one. "putttttth". She looked at me strange, but a smile was beginning to form on her face. She pulled and I "puttthh". Two came up; "puttthh", "puttthh". Her lips tightened as she tried to stifle a laugh. She pulled two more; "puttthh", "puttthh". She could barely contain the laugh now, as I knew I had her. This time I squatted down and began to pluck some of my own, very fast. "puttthh", "puttthh", "puttthh", "puttthh", "puttthh", "puttthh", "puttthh", "puttthh". Molly could contain it no longer, suddenly erupting into a barrage of giggles.

After a few hours of walking we sat down for a rest; our feet were bare and sore from the rocks and hard jagged ground, and me not fully recovered from my blood loss, exhaustion came early. Molly began to work with her collection of large white daisies, threading them together in a chain, much like I did to the dandy lions as a kid. Every now and then a snicker would come out as she worked. I moved my face closer to hers and stared looking for a reaction, but she continued to look down at her flowers working away at her chain. I kissed her forehead. The big smile that showed on her face just now certainly indicated some life, but the work continued. I made the sound once again for good measure, "puttthh." Molly's head went forward into her lap as a snicker burst its way out. What would it take, I wondered? She seems to have a wall built up much like mine, but it I could tell that it was slowly coming down.

Over a short distance from where we sat, I noticed a bush or vine with baseball sized orange fruit growing on it, or so I thought. Getting up, I went over to investigate. As I got closer I was immediately attacked by a strange odor hovering about the plant. The fruit looked like either oversized tangerines or maybe oranges, and I was hungry. I reached down, touched one and was about to pick it, when I finally got a reaction from Molly.

"Neea!" It seemed I was being warned. "Nata onee yada!" She got up and walked over to me at the bush. "Neea", she cried again pushing me back. Molly plucked one off the bush and put it on the ground. Looking around, she came back with a large flat rock, stepped back a few feet, then threw the rock on top of the fruit. SQUISH! She then waited for my reaction this time with a smile on her face. I carefully stepped closer to the smashed fruit for a look as Molly put her hand to her mouth and looked to be holding back a laugh.

"OH, OH WOW!" I stepped back quickly coughing and waving the air. What a smell! "What the heck are those?" I asked. "Oh man!" Molly was laughing to herself hysterically. "That is unbelievably foul! Nasty little things aren't they, just growing wild here and there, sheesh."

Finding a stick I proceeded to poke at an undamaged one still hanging on the vine. "Squirt." More of the foul stench filled the air. Giving it a tug I managed to pull it from the vine keeping it on the end of my stick. Molly watched with a bit of curiosity, that is until I moved closer to her face with it.

Squeaking, she ran as I then gave chase around the clearing and among the trees, both of us giggling.

"Ence!" she protested running to and fro. "Neea, netaday…, Ence!" We played for a few minutes, chasing around trees and such, feeling very much like children again, forgetting about the troubles of the day and simply enjoying ourselves in the moment. Finally, as she came out from among the trees and back into the clearing, she lost sight of me. As she was looking around to see just where I'd gone, I crept up behind her and grabbed my arms around her, picking her up off the ground. Giving out a scream that popped my ears, she struggled causing both to fall to the ground in a heap. We both laid there breathing hard and giggling, my arms still holding her tight.

"Hello," I said finally, still breathing.

"Good morning," she giggled.

I wanted very much to kiss her. But instead she put her hands on my chest, pushed herself up on her feet and gave me a coy smile as she walked over to her daisies. Picking up her chain she began to walk. "Yonaee," she called waving me over.

"Yip, time to go." Getting up I followed her. As I caught up to her I gave her a 'hip bump'. And with a big smile on her face she 'hip bumped' me back. No kisses yet, but I still had some hope. I reached down and took her hand.

As we walked, the clearing slowly disappeared as we found ourselves once again being closed in on all sides with the dense forest. Those nasty little orange stink vines were still present here and there and strangely enough they gave me an idea.

I began to wonder just how much she really understood. Was she having dreams about who I really am and where I came from? It's certainly far easier for me to understand Molly's life then she trying to make sense of a starship, me coming from another planet, or anything else about it. Picking two of the stink oranges, two rocks and a piece of tree bark, I was going to make an attempt. But as soon as I picked up the stink oranges Molly began to run in another direction.

"Molly!" I called after her. "Neea." I patted the ground as I sat down. She stopped, then looking a little confused she came and sat down next to me. "I wasn't going to chase you, I have something to show you." I held up a stink orange. "Sun," I said, tapping the orange and then pointing to the sun in the sky. "Sun," I repeated. Then with the other hand I picked up one of the rocks. "Maru." I then orbited Maru around the sun. Was she grasping the idea? Were they, as a people, already aware their world was round and circling the sun? I watched her as I went through my exhibit. I put the sun and Maru on the ground next to Molly and picked up the other orange. "Sun,"

Now we're getting to the 'new ideas' category. I picked up the other rock, "Earth." I kept watching her. "Earth," I then orbited Earth around its sun. Molly's face was changing expression as she observed my actions. I put Earth and its sun several feet away. "Vince...Earth," I said tapping my rock. I reached over and then tapped her rock, "Molly...Maru." I paused for a second to let it sink in a bit. Her face kept changing as she looked at the oranges and rocks. Molly picked up her orange and Maru and proceeded to orbit them on her own. There's no doubt how smart she is, I just wonder if this may be a bit beyond her grasp. I then reached for the piece of tree bark. "Vince," I said, making sure she had her eye on me. Then, making a swish sound with my mouth I sailed the tree bark from Earth to Maru. Molly looked at me, the tree bark, then the stink orange, her face painted with confusion.

Well, it was worth a try at least. I don't think there's any way to make her understand these concepts completely. It really won't work between she and I any way; too many differences, different cultures, different ways of life, the whole lot of it. I picked up her feet and began to rub them. This sparked another coy smile from her. I don't know who I was fooling, other than myself. I put this people through hell all because of my curiosity and loneliness. How will I ever repay these kind gentle folk.

I held Molly's feet up a bit, "Feet," I said. "Beautiful feet." And they were. They were the cutest little feet I've ever seen. I kissed the tops as I rubbed them. The look Molly was giving me just then was a look I've never seen before. She was giving me that same coy smile but in a way that seemed to mean, perhaps, a little more.

Just then my ears caught a sound that I have never heard before, that is, never heard before on Maru. I stood up and look toward the sound. At first I saw nothing, but then way off in the distance, two specks were flying just above the tree tops. As Molly got up to look I pointed. The specks seemed to be circling around here and there off in the distance.

"Scouts!" I hollered. "Pasarin Scouts, and I'll bet they're A-Meels, and they're looking for me." Pasarin scouts are one or two man shuttles, very fast and very maneuverable and, without a doubt, well armed. Knowing that scanners would not work in the E.M. zone, they were most likely searching by site alone. Desperate aren't they. I fully expected Molly to be frightened, to run and hide somewhere like a frightened quail, but like me she just stood there watching, seemingly without fear at all. She has seen these before apparently, they all have, at least for the last five years, which was the time, our good friend in the castle dungeon said A-Meel had first arrived. They had gotten used to seeing them from time to time it would seem. Maybe there's some hope of Molly understanding me after all.

We watched for a moment until it looked as if they were getting bigger as their sound also grew louder. Are they coming this way?

"Yip!" I declared alarmed, "they sure are. Let's go sugar!" I grabbed Molly's hand and took her out of the clearing and deeper into the thick trees. Crouching down in a ditch on the side of a hill we waited as we heard the screaming of the engines growing even louder.

There was no mistaking the sound. These type of engines always were noisy and had a distinctive resonance, announcing their presence long before you saw them. The Star Shark's engines were fairly quiet with the exception of a slight hum when they were close, which was certainly preferable when trying to approach covertly.

Soon the small shuttles roared over head above the trees where we sat, banking and fading out of sight over the hills beyond. But it wasn't long before the unmistakable sound grew louder again.

"Here they come for another pass!" I cried still holding on to Molly in the crevasse. I was beginning to think that maybe they found a way for their scanners to work in spite of the E.M. field and had indeed found us! The engines were again deafening as they roared past us over head. I saw them fade out of sight again as they passed, coming from another direction this time, they banked looking to be coming around yet again. A-Meel, apparently, is not one for giving up it seems.

Then without warning, they made an immediate course change, quickly darting off in another direction. Standing up I looked and watch them go. Were they called back? Did they give up? Then totally without warning, that hum in which I was oh so familiar, SWISH!

My heart pounded! "MOLLY! INTERCEPTORS!" I pointed toward the sky as I've never felt more alive than that moment. "Interceptors...from the Shark!" I screamed. I ran out of the ditch and back into the clearing for another look, Molly followed. "YEAH!" I screamed throwing a fist into the air. "Go Sam, Go!" It didn't take long before they were specks again fading over the hill. The interceptors, or W.A.S.P.S as they were called, were unmanned drones that were actually part of the Star Shark, and could be sent out on a variety of missions such as research, reconnaissance, aerial photography, or whatever, and could easily be used to search for me. And they were indeed armed to the teeth.

BOOOOM!! The horizon suddenly lit up the late evening with an explosion that was just out of sight, somewhere beyond the trees as the ground shook underneath out feet. Molly's eyes got big as she grabbed my arm and latched on.

"Ooo, I hope that was good news we just heard," I mumbled. We both stood there amazed as both the light and sound quickly subsided. "Well, one thing's for sure, the Shark is looking for us."

Our journey continued on with Molly leading the way, and I holding her hand in mine. Her hands seemed so small in comparison and yet they seemed to hold a power beyond what my hands ever would. Through our short but perilous journey in the wilderness, she was able to teach me things that only someone such as herself could teach. And as different and strange as we were to one another I knew that I could never let her go. My life had indeed changed in so many ways and she was very much an important part of that now.

We continued down the hill, through the trees into another clearing beyond. It was almost dark and I was hoping that maybe, just maybe, we wouldn't have to sleep out in the cold night again. She seemed to know just where she was going, and I hoped she also had plan.

Out of the corner of my eye I could see that she had been watching me, studying me as we walked along. Keeping my eyes ahead I pretended not to notice, but just kept walking, then smiling. I was nothing to look at really, especially with my face dirty, several days unshaven, no bath for a few days either, and nothing but an ugly pair of thin pants to wear, and my hair, who knows what that looks like. But with our special and sacred connection that we shared I hoped that she had been looking at me from the inside. I just hoped that my inside looked a darn sight better than what my outside did at the moment.

Suddenly Molly started to giggle. I turned to look at her as we walked, which seemed to make her giggle more. The more she looked at me the more she giggled.

"Ok," I said finally, "I give. What's the joke?" Her giggling just seemed to get worse. "You still thinkin' about the daisies or what?"

"Lowta," she said finally through her giggling. "Sena lowta." She reached up and put both her hands in my hair and lifted it up with her fingers. Her giggling suddenly when into hysterics.

"A flower." I shook my head. "Yes, I'll jet bet I look real hansom right now. You must be tired, you're gettin' silly." We kept walking. "Ya know my mom used to call me dahlia because of my poofy hair as a baby." I then began to laugh myself. Yes, it was funny. It was funny and I was glad because she seemed to be losing any shyness she may have had before. Molly continued her study of me, still giggling, her face beaming.

Finding ourselves in the middle of a small clearing I stopped and looked around for a moment. Taking Molly's left hand and putting it around my neck then taking her right hand with my left, I hummed what I could remember of a waltz and began to dance, turning and swinging her around as graceful as I could. Round and round we went looking into the other's eyes, shy smiles on our faces as we lost ourselves in the moment. My right hand was around her waist holding her tight still locked onto her eyes. Her pulse throbbed through my hand as my own heart was doing its own pounding on top of it. I had forgotten the feeling, it had been too long, or maybe I had blocked it all out a long time ago. But it all started to rush back to me now, as I began to feel very much like a young school kid all over again, like I was dancing for the first time. Round and round in a clearing we went, somewhere deep in the forest on a faraway planet in which I was not supposed be.

It was dark now and the breeze became cool, but we took no notice of it. We had the moon and the stars lighting our grass covered dance floor, the trees surrounding us as if playing the part of the audience in our grand ball room. There in our personal arena we turned and swayed and danced, gathering our memories together into one sacred moment when we could finally stand together and touch at last. Eventually our dance slowed as my humming faded. We were locked onto the other's eyes totally immersed, our hearts beating so fast now, as nothing else seemed to exist around us. I brought my face closer to hers and could feel her breathe again. It was so sensuous and yet so frightening at the same time, but I couldn't stop. "Oh my goodness," I thought, "What in the world am I doing?" I put both arms around her and held her close to me as Molly closed her eyes putting both her arms around my neck. "Somebody stop me before I make a big mistake." Ever so gently I pressed my lips to hers and held her there for some moments.

After the kiss Molly looked up at me still beaming, caressing my face with her hands. She looped her arm into mine and began to lead me once again through the now dark forest.

"Onta," she said pointing ahead. Between the trees I could barely make it out but, it appeared to be a small structure sitting there in the moon light.

"Awesome! Shelter for the night, too cool." I was still distracted, my mind in a fog thinking about the kiss. I can't believe I just kissed her. Doing more looking at Molly then down the path I suddenly slipped and fell into a creek that had snuck up on me. It wasn't very deep, maybe a few feet, just enough to get me soaking wet, yet again. Being drenched and staying that way seemed to be my lot on this trip. Molly stood there on the bank with her hand on her mouth trying not to laugh too loudly but laughing herself silly none the less. "It's ok," I said irritated, "you can laugh, I'm here to entertain, really." She gave me that 'poor, poor, man' look but continued to laugh till I thought she was going to split. Sitting up I reached my hand out for help out of the creek, but as she bent down to reach out to me, I took her by the hand and pulled her into the creek with me. SPLOOSH! A short scream later, she was now as wet as I, sitting beside me in the water with a look on her face that would certainly have killed any fish watching. I thought I was done for right then and there, but soon a snicker burst out, then a laugh. Any laughing I did, on my part, was mostly out of relief cause I wasn't sure that was the smartest thing to do.

Helping each other out of the creek, we made our way over to the small structure. "Cozy," I said, noticing its compact dimensions. It was no bigger than large tool shed, had no windows, but only a single door located on one side. "Better then a kick in the pants. By the way, how do you know about these little hide-a-way places anyway?" The answer to that mystery would not be unveiled till much later.

Molly went to the door and slowly pushed it open as a soft groaning came from its rusted hinges. "Eena onta de." Her voice reverberated slightly as she poked her head inside the waiting darkness for a look. "ack na." From the light of the moon through the open door, all that was found inside was several blankets in a pile on a ruff wood floor and not much else, not that we need much else really. Blankets to sleep on and shelter for the night would certainly do it. We each unfolded a blanket and picked out our side of the small cabin to sleep on, all while keeping an eye on the other one. The problem, although as of yet unsaid, was obvious; each wanted to sleep, but had no desire to sleep in soaking wet clothing. After fumbling nervously with the blankets wondering how to proceed on with the problem, I finally took the initiative and closed the door which then made it pitch black inside our little room. In the dark I heard Molly follow after me latching the door shut.

"There's a good Idea," I said. I then felt my way to one corner of the room, away from my dry blanket, removed my pants and proceeded to ring them out the best I could. This made a splattering sound, filling the dark around us. I then dropped them in another dry corner to deal with in the morning. A moment later I heard a similar sound across the room; Splatter...Slop. Splatter...slop. Oh yes, she has two items, I forgot. Feeling around on all fours I found my blanket and crawled in for the night. Man, is it dark in here, although realizing Molly's current state of dress right about now, I'd pay handsomely for a flashlight.

What I expected next was the sound of Molly wrestling with her blanket turning in for the night, but what I heard instead was; THUD, THUD, THUD, THUD.

"Molly, what in the world are you doing?"

THUD, THUD, THUD.

"Yena onta myonoeea ma one myoneea," THUD, THUD, THUD.

"Ok, glad I asked."

THUD, THUD, THUD, BOOM.

"Eea!" Suddenly the sound changed. Scrap, scrap, scraaaaap, ka-boom.

"What in the name of..." I couldn't resist it. Crawling out of my blankets, I felt around on the floor toward the strange sounds until my hands found it. "A hole?" I felt around a little more. Its square. It's a hatch, an escape hatch that seemed to go underground! "Rock n roll,"

"Rock n Roll," she echoed.

In case we needed a quick exit, I figured, good thinking. But how did she know it was there? I was beginning to have a lot of little questions that needed answering lately. She then put the cover back over the hole.

"Ooo!" I said startled, "watch the fingers." Then; scrap, scrap, scrap. She was trying to push the cover down and it was fitting tight so I gave her a hand with it, pushing it till it fit squarely back in place. As I helped her push the cover back down, my hands found hers in the dark. "Hello," I whispered. She just giggled a little and went back to her blanket. "Yes," I thought "good Idea." So I went back to my blanket and laid down as well.

Laying there on my back on the hard floor I could hear the breeze picking up a little as it brushed the little cabin outside. I could hear it in the tree tops that surrounded us along with some night time critters that came out to make their own unique sounds. But my mind kept going back to Molly and what took place over the last twenty four hours. I can't believe I kissed her. I closed my eyes and tried to relax and letting my thoughts wonder. Just then images came to my mind, images of stringed flowers in some sort of ritual, I saw kissing, I also saw hands together with flowers wrapped around them. It appears I was getting thoughts from Molly. Other thoughts and feelings entered my mind as well, along with more images and things that I would need time to sort out. But apparently she was deep in thought about the whole affair, as she lay there, as I obviously was right now. The connection we shared seemed to be getting stronger the more time we spent together.

After listening in on Molly's thoughts awhile it came to me. I was seeing images of a bonding, a pairing, or 'the claiming' as these people called it. The word marriage didn't seem to be in their vocabulary but the essence of a marriage certainly did exist. The flower chain Molly was making, was for the ritual of 'the claiming', which the women did when they needed a man. The union then lasted a life time or until one of them died. Divorce was strictly forbidden here and carried a harsh punishment. In this I also learned, that a kiss, such as the one I gave Molly, in essence, sealed the deal. By kissing the lady, the gentlemen was agreeing to the union, like a signature on a contract, and in fact, this was enforceable by their law.

I began to wonder if I wasn't duped in some way into kissing her or desiring her by some magic spell or other. Just then, what George used to say to me, whenever I would get into scraps and such, echoed in my mind. He would say, "You just can't seem to stay out of trouble can you?" I guess he was right. How'd I get into this anyway? I do believe, However, that something brought us together, and I believed, whatever it was, could be found here on Maru, which would make Molly as much a victim in this as I. Besides, I did in fact love her, and to that there was no doubt.

"Hey Molly," I whispered.

"Eea sena," came back from somewhere in the dark.

"What cha doin'?"

"Ya nao oa," Molly giggled.

"Chatter, chatter, chatter."

"Eena, eena, eena," she giggled some more. Both of us were feeling good, giddy, and child like. I seemed to have a glow inside of me now that I couldn't get rid of.

"Puttttth." Making that sound again caused Molly laugh out loud.

She attempted to make the sound herself, "pthth", then laughed.

Crawling out of my blanket I slowly I went up to her head and put my hands on both sides of her face, touching my nose to hers.

"Hello."

"Good morning," she giggled some more.

"It's good evening," I said gently, "or in this case good night" Then gently and passionately I kissed her.

"Ence…, Neea."

"I know," I said whispering back to her with my lips just barely touching hers. "I'm treading on dangerous ground. But don't worry, I'm still a gentlemen. It's too dark, didn't see a thing." I then put my cheek next to hers with my mouth to her ear and whispered very slowly; "I…love…you." I kissed her again then went back to my blanket. Yeah that was a little dangerous, I certainly don't need a list of things to repent of. Time to cool down.

As I laid back down and did the best one could to get comfortable on a hard floor, I was met with soft hands searching for my face, then a kiss. Wow, Molly came to me for a kiss. "Rock n Roll." Another giggle came from somewhere in the dark. My mind drifted off again and slowly I went to sleep.

Suddenly, both of us were jolted awake with great alarm! BAM!…BAM!…"Molly!" I shouted in half asleep panic. BAM! Somebody was trying to break through the door! Within seconds Molly found the hatch in the floor again and started pulling in the dark.

"Yona onta metoa!" She screamed, as once again, she found herself fighting for her life.

BAM!…BAM! The banging outside continued. I heard the floor hatch open with a Ka-thud, and Molly scrambling down the hole. Still unable to see, I was scrambling about trying gather up the important things and follow Molly down the hole. But before I did, I placed two stink oranges on the floor directly in front of the door, took the cover to the hatch and slammed the oranges, then dropped out of sight pulling the cover on top of me. As I pulled the cover shut, I made sure that one of the blankets was covering the hatch as to, hopefully, hide the existence of the hole in the floor from our pursuers. A ladder clung to one side of the pit and continued down to an unseen bottom. As I worked my way down the ladder in the black, I suddenly felt Molly brush past me back up the ladder to the hatch again. "Whoa!" I jerked startled. "Almost knocked me off!" She locked the floor hatch in place and then climbed back down again.

"Ah," I said realizing what she had done. "There's a dandy idea." As I felt Molly brush past me in the dark I realized something else. "And by the way lady, haven't you forgotten something?"

BAM! CRACK! CRACK! It sounded like they made their way inside the cabin. We'd better get moving, and fast.

Following Molly down the ladder, I eventually found the bottom but, in the dark that's all I did find, along with the narrow sides of the hole, nothing else. Where did she go?! "Molly!" I called, in a bit of a panic, knowing that at any moment the floor hatch above me may be discovered.

"Ence!" Molly's voice echoing from somewhere in the empty black. I crouched down. My hands then found a small tunnel just big enough for one to crawl through if I got on my hands and knees. Letting out a big sigh I began to crawl, working my way through the cramped, dark, claustrophobic passage, which seemed to narrow in places as well as turn and twist.

"Molly!" I called out as I clawed my way through the dirt. I'm sure I'm going, wind up with some sort of phobia when I finally get outta here. I feel like I'm being buried alive. "How long is this tunnel anyway?" I hollered out. The tunnel suddenly got very short and narrow. "Crap!."

"Su ta!" Molly called back. "Ya no eea natosa."

"Yeah, you said it honey. Whew!" The tunnel went up, then it went down, twisting left then right, crazy death trap seemed to go on forever. Then the sound of water. It wasn't enough I was crawling around in a tunnel underground in the pitch black, now water.

Suddenly the floor of the tunnel dropped away. "Whoa!" I stopped short of falling in, then felt around. The tunnel stops here and goes down into a watery abyss. Molly's head popped up out of the water startling me.

"Ence! Su ta! She blurted breathing hard. She took a deep breath then disappeared in the water again.

"Ok, no place to go but down. How many phobias can you name now?" I took a deep breath and dropped down the dark watery hole. Grabbing the sides of the pit I then forced myself down deeper and deeper which, so far, appeared to have no bottom.

"Stay calm," I told myself. "You can do this." Then the walls of the pit disappeared, with nothing around me but water and black. Just as I was about to double back and make a break for the surface again, mostly from panic, a hand grabbed my arm and began to pull. As the hand pulled at me, I swam with it and soon began to see some light above. It was faint but it gave me some well needed consolation. In moments my head burst the surface into a moon lit night, as I took in a fresh gulp of air.

"Oh wow, that was a trip," I breathed with much relief. "Thank you my dear. Pretty clever little escape route you have there." As I pulled myself up on the bank and sat to breath a bit, I noticed that Molly stayed in the water wading with only her head showing above the surface. I knew why, but decided to play with her a bit. "That was too freaky. I hope we don't wind up having to go back the other way."

The tunnel appeared to come out into a pond of sorts, a deep one at that, located some distance from the cabin behind a hill, but as freaky as that tunnel was, I still wasn't sure that our pursuers haven't found their way though and I fully expected to have hands suddenly grab us from underneath the water.

"Let's go pretty lady," I told her standing up. "We may have come company any minute." I held out my hand to her, but at the moment, she seem quite contented to just sit there in the water. "Molly, come on." I waved my arm trying to coax her out, but Molly didn't move. She had a sheepish look on her face and even looked to shrink, a little more, in the water. I walked over to the edge and squatted down. "What's the matter?" I asked holding my hand out for her again.

"Na inshee eenini," she whined softy.

"I'm sorry, what?" I put my hand to my ear.

"Eenini." The guilt on her face was growing with intensity.

"Eenini?" Even in the weak moon light I could see the red face she had. I knew exactly what the problem was and was literally asking for the lightning to strike, but I couldn't resist the 'once in a life time' moment. In her panic she had rushed down the hatch forgetting something very important. I hoped she would discover her dilemma somewhere between the little cabin and the pond, and then wanted to see what her reaction would be.

Molly waited for a moment before responding, but then with a look of embarrassment she sat up out of the water for just a split second and just far enough to make her point then back down in the water to hide. "WHOA! Eenini!" I pretended to be surprised. "Molly eenini?" I gave out a chuckle. As her face turned even more embarrassed and angry she splashed some water up me. I put my arm up as if to block the moist attack still laughing. She just sat there with a look that would burn steal. Walking part way back into the water I pulled a bulge out from the back of my pants and handed it to her. It was her skirt. I remembered our clothes even if she forgot in all the panic. "Beautiful Molly." I said to her softly giving her a big smile. "You thought you'd have to do some hiking in the buff, didn't ya?" Her look softened while showing a great deal of relief as she took the skirt from me and put it on while still neck deep in the water. I then stepped out of the water and stood back from the pond a few feet, turned and looked at her. Molly sat there in the water looking at me with a smirk growing on her face, the whole thing becoming totally obvious. Then with a look that said, "Get a grip buddy," she stuck her hand out waiting for the top she knew I had. I reached back and pulled the other bulge out from the back of my pants and held the rolled up wad out as if wanting her to step out of the water and get it.

"Neea," she said, sounding irritated but with the smirk still on her face. I then unrolled the wad, opened it and held it out as if to help her put on, stepping only a couple more feet closer to the water. That definitely would not work either, as she remained hidden in the water with her hand out, her face still showing the smirk. "Ence, ya ne sha." This time I walked clear up the water's edge still holding the jacket open for her to come up and slip her arms in. Still giving me that "not going to happen" look, she just sat there her hand still out waiting for her jacket. I squatted down holding the jacket open for her. Molly remained frozen. Giving up I finally threw her the jacket. It was worth a try. With her head as the only thing showing above the water she slipped the jacket on, buttoning it up before she stepped out onto the grass next to me, her face now sporting a very coy smile.

"Soaking wet again," I held out my elbow for her. "I swear I'm gonna grow gills. I guess we'd better get going." As she looped her arm in mine, I pulled her close and kissed on the cheek.

Over the hill in the distance I could hear dogs barking from the direction of the cabin! I grabbed Molly's hand and we began to run!

CHAPTER ELEVEN

TRAPPED!

"Here we go again," I hollered, aiming for the thick of the forest with Molly in tow. "By the way, you're welcome…," we dashed over bushes and around trees, "…for remembering your clothes. I mean without me you'd be…well…," We bounded over rocks and down an embankment as fast as we could go, "…naked, eenini. Not that I would mind, I mean…"

"Eenini?" Molly asked panting. She obviously wasn't picking up my conversation. We were beginning to breath hard and as for myself, very wet and cold. "Ence eenini?".

"No, no, neea," I chuckled deciding to stop and look around for a moment. "Never mind." I bent over with my hands on my knees and tried to catch my breath. "Sorry, beautiful, I guess I'm not fully recovered yet. Either that or I'm beginning to feel my age."

I stood up and put my finger to my mouth. "Shhhh," We both listened for a minute to the wind in the trees and a few small critters, but otherwise it was fairly quiet. "We must've lost 'em. Dogs lost the scent at the cabin I figure, they must've taken another direction."

Deciding take a rest, I sat on the ground by a large tree. "Just as well to stay here for a while," I told her. "See if they won't wonder off somewhere else. Should be only an hour or so till day light really." I sat back against a large tree and tried to relax but being soaking wet and wearing only a thin pair of pants didn't make it easy, I was freezing in the cold night air. Molly sat down against a neighboring tree. "What in the world are ya sittin' clear over there for?" I patted the ground next to me and held out my arms for her. She being soaking wet as well, could certainly benefit from a bit of warming I thought. She got up and moved over next to me and slowly put her arms around me as we tried to keep each other warm. Molly felt so good in my arms as I held her close, I sat there for a while quite contented.

"So," I chirped, making Molly jump. Her face was hard to see in the dark which certainly added to the romance. "What did that mean when you said yesterday…what was it…a… 'Sena ottun', or something like that?"

"Sena ottun," Molly said giggling.

"Yes, what does that mean? Sena ottun. What is that?" For two people who spoke only a few words of each other's language we seemed to be doing ok.

Suddenly a light came on for her, as she then patted her behind. "Ottun."

"Ahhh, I see…, yer cabboose. 'Ottun' means yer cabboose, and 'sena' must mean nice, or something like that…, I hope? Maybe?" I laughed a bit. "So you think I have a nice cabboose eh?" I put my face right up to hers, remembering the incident with the blanket at the cave.

"Ence yano sena ottun," she whispered giggling.

"I see. I never got to see your ottun, not very fair at all?" I kissed her. She was all smiles and a little embarrassed. "Molly sena ottun?"

She giggled at that. "Neea."

I kissed her again. "Whaddya mean neea? What's this neea stuff, hmm?" Another kiss. "Molly sena ottun."

"Neea, neea," she whispered as her lips came for me this time, her arms tightening around me.

"Oh eea, eea," I whispered back to her as our lips came together once again and stayed that way for some time warming each other up quite nicely.

*   *   *   *   *   *

The early morning sun woke me as it drilled into my eyes, through the trees, pulling them open. Molly was laying on my shoulder with one arm and a leg draped over me, still sound asleep. I let her sleep on not wanting to move and wake her as I was enjoying every second just laying there holding her.

Soon, however she woke and we were on our way again, after having eaten the usual breakfast of leaves, stems, berries, and a few unrecognizable items. Once again she began to collect flowers.

"My kingdom for a cheese burger," I sighed as we walked together hand in hand, resuming our trek. "Oh yes, and a pair of shoes. Never again will I make fun of your…sandal-shoe things." I doubt Molly even got a small part of what I was trying to say to her, as I chattered on, but somehow I figured she didn't mind too much. If nothing else we still had our special connection going on, and that often times said more than we might put into words anyway. But, eventually, one of us is going to need to learn the language of the other if this unique relationship is going to work at all.

Just then something on the ground caught my eye. There were wooden boards laying side by side with a cross member connecting them together to form a square about four feet by four feet and was partial covered with leaves, dead tree limbs, and dirt. "What in the world?" Looking around, I saw a few more of these strange things placed here and there over a wide area, here among the trees. Bending down, I tried to lift it but found it would even budge an inch. I then knelt on it, putting my eyes down to see if I could peek between the boards as my insatiable curiosity, once again began to take over. CRACK!! The boards suddenly gave way as they splintered into fragments causing me to fall through barely catching myself on a remaining plank before plunging deep into the abyss far below. Molly gave out a screamed as she got on her hands and knees beside the pit.

"Ence!"

"Molly!" I screamed, gripping the last unbroken board with all my strength. As I attempted to pull myself up the board began to crack. I froze! "Oooh crap." I dared not breathe. In a total state of panic Molly moved around the square pit tryin to figure what to do next. As she reached for my hands the boards in a neighboring hole gave way as well. CRACK!! She screamed as she fell just catching the remaining board and saving herself from taking the deep plunge as well. As we both hung there we could see each other as the holes opened up into a large cavern. I watched Molly struggle for a hand hold as the board she was hanging on to became loose on one end. "Don't move!" I warned her. "Molly, don't move!" She seemed to understand as she stopped her struggling.

Then a sound came from somewhere above us. "Molly," I whispered loudly. "Shhhh." She stopped her whimpering for a moment and listened. Talking. We heard talking and footsteps thought the brush. "Shhh," I whispered again, "Don't move." The talking and footsteps got louder until they seemed to be right on top of us for a moment and then began to fade. The board I was hanging on to, sagged a little more a gave out a small cracking sound. "Please, please, please!"

After what seemed like forever the sounds from above eventually faded, I figured it was now or never to try and pull myself out. If I didn't soon, I certainly was going to find out where the bottom was, the hard way.

It's interesting how strange thoughts enter your head at certain moments when you should be thinking about the task at hand, especially when you're about to drop to your death. "Ya know," I told Molly as we both hung there by our hands seconds away from death, "that's the first time I've seen your belly button." I watched her jacket being hiked up because her arms reaching upwards as she griped the board with all her life. She stared at me with big freighted eyes as if to say, "Well, get us out of this, you moron!" But then I noticed her skirt slipping. It was never meant to be a shirt, it was a full dress that she had ripped the top off of because one of the guards had ripped it back in the castle. And now it was slipping down a little below her hips.

She resumed her whimpering as she lifted her knees up in an effort to keep the dress from slipping away completely. I tilted my head sideways staring being mesmerized at the sight that was hanging before me.

"ENCE!" She shouted with an angry glare.

"What? Right, sorry." I shook myself back to reality and went back to work. Slowly and carefully I moved hand over hand to the edge to the pit where two boards came together in the corner and began pulling myself up. The board then gave a heavy crack. Hanging my your fingers has a nasty way of draining any strength that you may have had, making the task that much more difficult in the end. I pulled and strained, grabbing on to grass, weeds and anything that came within my reach. I finally was able to swing my leg up and pull myself out of the pit. "Whew." No time for rest as I quickly went over to the hole where my sweet Molly was hanging and I began to coax her over.

"Molly! Right here," I patted the corner of the pit. "Slowly, just like I did." As she slowly began to move her hands over, the corner of the board she was hanging on loosened a bit more. "Come on, you can do it." Whimpering and struggling she finally made it over. Just as I grabbed both her arms the board finally came loose and fell into the black below. Molly gave out a scream as she tightened her grip on my arms. With what little strength I had left I pulled and pulled at her arms, and ever so slowly began to drag her out of the gaping abyss. She was unable to swing her legs up as her skirt was now restricting her movement. This meant that if she was going to make it out alive, I had to use all of my own strength without her help. Molly had only to hang on to me as tight as she could. Pulling and pulling I went until I thought I was going to pull her arms right out of her sockets. Quickly I then grabbed underneath her arm pits and repositioned my feet for better leverage. I gave a hard pull, and up she came collapsing on top of me as I laid on my back. "Whew!" We both just laid there for a moment breathing, she with her head on my chest, both of us very glad to be alive. I put my arms around her and kiss her.

"Almost lost ya lady," We both just laid there for a moment as I held her tight. "Ya know, you guys might wanna check out the bloomer idea. I'm just sayin." I just saved her life, which I guess makes us even. She didn't seem to care at the moment however, she was just glad to be alive.

Eventually I got up and decided to take a closer look at the holes. "Ya know, these look old," I peered carefully back down into the traps. "They look to have been here long before A-Meel arrived. Looks like an old mine of sorts. Curious." Was there somebody else around who also believed there was a huge load of polynesium here and tried to find it? But who? I reached out for Molly. "We'd better go completely around. Even the ground between these traps looks weak and I ain't gonna take a chance." Putting my hand around her waist I walked with her avoiding the holes and the ground surrounding them. I then put my mouth to her ear and whispered. "Sena ottun." Molly looked up with an embarrassed smile.

Our journey continued on through a field of flowers which Molly began to collect without hesitation. We hung around in the field until she was happy with the length of the new flower chain. Then picking a spot in the middle of the field she knelt down.

"Ence," She called out, patting the ground in front of her, large flower chain in hand. Just then, I got a strange feeling inside, is she doing what I think she's doing? The images I got from Molly much earlier, made the scene very familiar, and I believed I had a small idea what was about to take place. Complying to her request, I came over and knelt down with her. Yes, I'm a little frightened, who wouldn't be. I've gotten myself in deep and the laws of the land here are clear, besides, there is absolutely no way, that I can see, to just fly away and forget her, nor would I want to.

Molly took my left arm and held it out and began to wrap her flower chain around it starting at the elbow. At that point she put the palm of her right hand on my left palm and continued to wrap our hands together. The chain then continued up her arm to her elbow. We were linked in a chain of flowers, a scene which I remembered seeing in Molly's mind. Whatever is about to take place here, right now, right at this moment is going to be permanent, and I knew that. My heart began to beat wildly. She then took my right hand in her left, closed her eyes, bowed her head, and began to speak. What she was saying I had no way of knowing, but after she was done speaking, she then bade me to repeat it word for word, in the same manner. I did as she bade, and with her help I repeated it until I spoke it word for word as she did. The whole process taking a good ten minutes partially due to my difficulty in pronouncing the words in her language, but after this was all done, she looked at me with a big smile and a glow. I was about to lean over and kiss her, thinking that was the end but was stopped as she put her fingers on my mouth. I would later learn that kissing was not allowed, that is not yet, as this was only step one of a very personal, and very sacred ritual, one that had been handed down through the ages.

Not far from the field of flowers, where we were kneeling, was a stone house with a wood frame sitting by itself among the trees. We had finally reached the edge of the village, after a few days of walking with sore bare feet, hunger, thirst, and exposure, and all that we had been though, we had actually made it, although this house was located on the outskirts of the village and we still had a ways to go to get back to Molly's family. Holding hands with our arms still wrapped with the flower we approached the house only to stop with sudden horror as we saw two guards walk out the front door. Molly and I quickly dove in a nearby ditch and hid. Did they see us? Obviously they haven't stopped searching, and they do seem to have an irritating knack for knowing our general whereabouts. We watched the two guards mount their horses and ride away, but sat hiding for a few moments more just in case there may be others still in the house. As the guards finally road out of sight Molly and I stepped out of the ditch and approached the house. She let go of me and charged the door as I followed her in. Did she know these people? Small village like this, I would guess everybody knows everybody.

An older looking lady came into the room as I stood by the front door. I was suddenly aware of my lack of good clothes and how dirty I must look. But the lady of the house didn't seem to notice as she and Molly greeted each other loudly and hugged each other. Yip, I guess they do know each other. The lady looked Molly up and down then me as Molly appeared to be explaining the adventures she and I had just been through over the last few days. She held up the flowers and pointed to me, which started another round of hugs. The old lady approached me and began to chat with me taking my hand, but Molly interrupted her. Most likely to explain the language difference to her. It feels very strange to be on the other side of the barrier, being the one that doesn't understand the lingo. It makes one feel a little left out and lost. But then, I've learned that, in this situation, one will be ok, if one just goes with the flow, so to speak. And that's what I did, although learning the language will definitely be on my 'to-do' list.

Molly and I were then led down stairs to the cellar into a room that contained mostly shelves cluttered with odd items, as other strange objects were scattered about here and there on the floor. And there in the middle of the room was a large wooden tub. Our host then left us briefly and came back with some washing cloths and towels that she then set out on a table that stood along one wall. Peaking behind a curtain in a doorway I found a second room which had a bed, a small table and more shelving. The lady then led Molly into that room and showed her a small hidden hatch in the wall that lay behind some movable shelving. "Awesome," I thought. "In case our friends come back we'll have some place to go." No doubt this was another safe house, a great risk the lady had take on to herself. I wondered how many she had help in the last few years and where they all went from here. A dangerous business if she's ever found out. "I hope that doesn't go to another pond like the last one." I thought to myself as looked down the tunnel. "One of those was more than enough."

Our host left again and came back with a bucket in each hand full of water and began to fill the large tub. Right away I employed myself to give her an hand and between the three of us we managed to fill the tub in about fifteen minutes drawing the water from a well outside in the back of the house. The old lady then left the room and close the door behind her.

I looked at Molly, and she looked at me a big smile dressing her face, we were alone in the room. Right now I'm lost at what to do. Do I wait in the other room to let her bath first or what. I was about to do just that when Molly took me by the arm and stood me in front of the tub. On the table with the towels our host also brought down some herbs and things in bowls, for what purpose I was shortly about to discover. I did, however recognize the animal fat soap in a bowl that sat near the big wooden tub.

As I was thus looking around the room I was suddenly startled by Molly as she dropped my pants to the floor and took them away from me. Step two in the process of 'the bonding' or 'the claiming'; the cleansing to start anew. Starting the marriage off with, quite literally, a clean start. This also served to represent service to each other within the lifetime of the marriage as each learns to serve the other in everything they do. I said nothing as she proceeded to bath me as I stood there, starting with my hair then downward. After rinsing and drying me off and rubbing the appropriate herbs in all the right places, I then did the same for her. I then understood why the ritual of marriage here on Maru was a very private and sacred affair, unlike marriages on earth where everybody attends and celebrates. Here that definitely would not be the case, for obvious reasons. There was, however, a feast organized on behalf of the couple at some point afterwards in which family, relatives and friends would then attend and celebrate the new union.

Step three, and the finally step; the confirmation. Molly then led me back to the small room with the spare bed in it and drew the curtains closed in the doorway. She then went to a small window high on the wall and opened it up to let as much sunshine as she could in the room, a strange but apparently necessary part of the ritual involved sunshine.

Later that afternoon, we found that our host had laid out for us new clothes in the wash room. "Rock n roll," I said noticing a real shirt, Maruin style, but a shirt, complete with a new pair of pants. "And shoes! Oh yes! Boots even! Oh man I missed having shoes."

"Rock n roll," Molly echoed holding up a new dress. It was an old dress that the lady of the house had given her to replace the torn one that Molly was wearing, but a whole dress none the less. Once I am able to get back to the Star Shark I'm going to give her all the dresses she would ever want.

As we finished dressing in our new clothing, we heard the old lady holler something from upstairs, Molly then gave a response hollering back. As I got up and helped her tie up her dress in the back Molly turned around to me. "Yehne," she said, pointing up the stairs. I remember. I think that means food, or eat. The lady of the house had fixed us some food.

"Rock n roll!" I patted my stomach. Then it dawned on me like a load of bricks falling from the ceiling; I was married. I was actually married. I did it. I looked at her, as she fussed with her apron, she was so beautiful, so awesome. But what a marriage it was going to be. I couldn't even speak her language, and the rituals and all customs I would have to learn! Could I do it? Would I have to give up the Shark? What was it going to be like? Well, I definitely had all the time in the world to learn, and I was just going to take it one day at a time.

Just then another sound came from upstairs, this time it sounded kinda like a short scream that was suddenly silenced. I pushed Molly into the bed room behind the curtain and then went back and put my back against the wall. Slowly I began to peak around the corner up the stairs. Shadows on the wall were slowly and ever so quietly working their way down the stairs toward us. My heart began to pound. "Shhhh," Ever so quickly I went into the bedroom, opened the secret hatch in the wall behind the shelves and pushed Molly in.

"Ence?" she whispered back, panic growing on her face again.

"Guards!" I whisper back. Her eyes went great big as she scrambled in the tunnel. When she saw I wasn't coming with her, she crawled back and grabbed my arm.

"Ence! Ee no aya," Becoming frantic and more than a little confused, she began to cry. She could plainly sense my emotions, but there was no time to explain.

"Go, go!" I insisted as I pushed her hands out of the way and closed the hatch. Pushing the shelves back in place preventing her from coming back out, I then hid the hatch again. All the while I could hear her knocking on the hatch door, crying.

"Ence! Ence!" she said in tears, muffled by the hatch door and the shelving. My heart was breaking, but there was no time.

I went back to the stairway and pressed my back up against the wall as suddenly a guard stepped into the room. With my right, I back handed him as hard as I could in the throat. As he went down I grabbed his sword from his scabbard. Inside the tunnel Molly still sat there next to the hatch with her hands to her mouth, tears in her eyes, fear and rage on her face. She held quiet as she could, as her body shook with fright. The next guard swung his sword around the corner at me, I bent over as his sword hit the wall. With my sword now in hand I turned it toward the next attacker and rammed it in his stomach just under his breast plate then pulled it back out again. Another one collapsed to the floor. Suddenly a crossbow fired an arrow around the corner at me. Still ducking it went into the bedroom and hit the far wall. Moving to the middle of the room, I poised my sword.

CHAPTER TWELVE

DISCOVERY

"Oh crap," I gaped, looking up the stairs seeing six more guards, all coming down into the cellar with me and I had no way out. As they flooded in around me I stepped back and tripped on the large wooden tub and fell to the floor on my back. The guards, taking advantage of this, poured in on top of me. I couldn't move except to manage a kick, sending one guard smashing to a wall. The rest piled on top of me penning me to the floor and began to beat the living daylights out of me. Moments later I lost consciousness.

As I woke, I found myself on my stomach with my hands tied behind my back and my feet also tied together with my hands, my head and ribs throbbing with pain from the beating. I appeared to be on a horse drawn wagon, headed back to the castle, I presumed. I knew I had to make my way back, somehow, to try and keep the reactor from blowing it's top killing possibly hundreds or even thousands more, and this was a good a way as any, although I could have done without the beating. Somebody had to stop that maniac, A-Meel, from doing what he was doing to this planet and these people and since I felt I was the one that started this whole mess I elected myself as the lucky candidate to get the job done. Besides who else knew how to do it!

I looked around and saw two guards riding up front on the wagon with me, the rest were on horses following. I listened to them chattering back and forth and realized another important fact; these were not Pasarin. They were speaking the Maruin language. The realization that came to me just then was a bit shocking considering the nature of these peaceful people. How could any Maruin man even consider leaving his wife and family to participate in their own destruction? Knowing what I do about their customs, laws, and beliefs it made no since what so ever. I looked them over as they road, fine clothes, silver and gold chest plates and swords. Without a doubt, they were most likely bribed and then promised more if they helped in A-Meel's cause, and the rest of the men who refused to be a part of it? They were sent down to the mines. Pure speculation for sure, but what else would fit? As the full extent of what was happening to this people became clearer, both my gilt and rage grew.

Just then my thoughts were interrupted. I felt Molly in my mind, her rage and fear came flooding back to me. She had been tracking me, mentally keeping tabs on me and my well being. Everything that I had discovered and had been thinking just now she had been hearing.

Then something strange happened. Words in Maru came to my mind as well as their meaning along with the rage that sent them. I then repeated aloud the words, that came to my mind, making sure the guards could hear me.

"Ye te ohna ra otora!" I spoke with my teeth clenched as I could feel Molly's rage pouring back to me as she spoke to the guards through me. The chattering between the guards suddenly stopped as one of them turned to look at me with surprise on his face. I don't think they were expecting me to speak to them in their own tongue, somehow. I continued;

"You traitorous otora! How could you even think to abandon your wives and your children and to make them go hungry while you seek after selfishness that was promised to you by the lies of an off-worlder!" The thoughts stopped coming, but I could still feel the anger pouring in from Molly. Wow, that was wild! And definitely a first! I laid there on my stomach in the back of their wagon silent now, listening. The guards spoke not a word after that but remained quiet for the duration of our little trip.

Eventually the wagon stopped. Still bound like a wild animal, I was lifted off the wagon and carried down into a large cave. Deeper and deeper we went until finally I was thrown down onto the hard rocky ground. Untying my feet and hands the guards then pushed me down a rocky slope.

Gaining my feet I was met with an amazing spectacle. Instantly I was taken aback at what I was seeing. I had been taken to a large cavern with tunnels jutting out in all directions from a massive central hub. But what was even more startling was the men that I found there, hundreds of them pounding and chipping away at the rock with sledge hammers and picks then hauling the rock away by buckets. They had torn ragged clothing, and were dirty and bruised, some bleeding. Suddenly a loud "SNAP!" echoed across the large vista with flash then a cry of pain. "SNAP!" Another flash somewhere else and another cry of pain. Guards were using some sort of weapon to keep the workers in line and working. "Found 'em," I whispered horrified. It was a horrible sight watching the men of Maru being slowing driven to their deaths, all in the search for one very powerful rock.

"SNAP!" My right leg was suddenly filled with sharp pain causing me to collapse to one knee as a sledge hammer came bounding toward me barely missing my head. As I picked it up

I was given a heavy shove toward where others were at work. Limping over began to pound away with them.

After working away at the rock for a while, waiting for the guards to move on elsewhere, I Looked around the gigantic cavern and began counting the number of guards. We had them out numbered twenty to one easy, or better. If it wasn't for those blasted laser weapons frightening the willies out of them we could easily over whelm them. But the problem would be to convince a people to go up against a technology they have never seen before, a technology that is outside their current understanding. Yet if there was a chance at all I had to take it, and it may mean getting zapped a few more times.

I continued to hammer away for awhile giving some thought to an idea that I had brewing. Over to my right, a middle aged looking man also stood pounding away with his hammer. All these guys looked half dead. I looked around as I hammered away trying not to temp the guards with the laser again. Some of the guards were coming and going through a short tunnel a few hundred yards away behind me. I turned briefly to look then went back to work. An elevator! If we are indeed below the castle, like I thought I saw, then that's the way. A diversion, I would need a diversion and a large one. If I could create a diversion large enough that would allow the people to free themselves by mobbing out the main tunnel, that should keep the guards busy and allow me to make a dash for the elevator and find that make-shift reactor, hopefully before it blows us all into a high orbit. But what would scare them more then the lasers. Looking up I saw the answer. Three huge pipes running the length of the cavern high on the ceiling. Water!" Has to be. That's where the river is diverted from the river to cool the reactor chamber which is right about..., I followed the pipes with my eyes. There. Taking my sledge hammer I moved to a location directly under the pipes, and started to pound.

"Ooya na," I said turning to a man chipping away close to me. In Maru that means 'hello' or 'goodbye'. It could even mean 'thank you' when used that way. Directly translated it means; 'Grace to you."

"Ooya na," he mumbled back without breaking the rhythm of his pick. I looked up at the pipes.

"A little high, but I think I can do it." I pounded some more on the rocks as I looked around for the guards. Removing one of the watches that remained hidden underneath my long sleeve, I put it in my hand and resumed my work again. Funny thing about polynesium. Use it right and it's a miracle. Pushing a series of buttons on the watch, I set it for a five minute count down. Use it wrong and It will bite you, and bite big. Looking around for the guards and holding the watch bottom side up I then flung the watch as hard as I could at the pipes over head. As the watch sailed in the air, it came within an inch of the pipes and fell back. Catching it, I quickly went back to work, waiting for the next safe opportunity. When it came, I reset the timer and gave another throw. Up it went, hitting the pipe wrong side up, then down it came. As I caught it a second time, a guard walked over then stopped, eyeballing my group, his laser at the ready. Did he see me? Still hiding my watch in the palm of my hand as I gripped the hammer, I continued my labor at the stone. The guard didn't move, he just stood there looking around, watching us as we pounded away, while the timer in my hand continued its count down. If I don't find a way to either reset the timer or put a stop to it, without him seeing me, we're going to have a big problem, or I should say I'M going to have a big problem. My heart began to beat heavily as few more moments went by. I wrestled the watch around in my hand while trying to avoid missing my gait with the sledge hammer, trying to feel which button is which, without actually looking at it. As this moment, I could either save my own life or lose it in an easy mistake. I think I found it. As I kept working the hammer, I pushed a button. Sweating out a few more moments I waited, keeping my hammer going. Well, I'm still here, now if that big ugly guard would just leave I could do this. Slowly sauntering over to another area, he finally left. As soon as he was far enough away, and for the moment no other guards had their eyes on us, I looked at the watch. The timer read two seconds. I quietly breathed out and reset it. Holding it bottom up once again, I heaved it up toward the over head pipes once more. "Clank" It stuck, magnetized to the metal of the pipe. Back to work with the sledge hammer. "Ok," I told myself. "You've got less than five minutes."

I then began to chant softly with each pound of my hammer; "Neea…, neea." I nudged the guy next to me and continued to chant. "Neea…, neea." He gave me a strange look but I kept up the chant, "Neea…, neea."

He then joined in. "Neea…, neea." The guys on the other sides of us looked as though we gone crazy. "Neea…, neea." Then the light came on for them as well. "Neea…, neea." Within a minute, our whole section was doing the chant. "Neea…, neea." This began to create a stir among the guards, but what could they do? We were still working hard, pounding with each beat of the chant. "Neea…, neea." Then within three minutes most of the cavern echoed with the chant. "Neea…, neea…, neea…, neea." the guards were at a loss.

"Come guys," I thought to myself as I chanted. "Think about it."

"Neea…, neea…, neea…, neea."

Then without warning; *BOOOM*! My watch had blown a fairly large crack in one of the pipes over head. Water began to surge out causing the crack to widen which then caused a deluge to come pouring out into the cavern.

Anarchy and chaos took over as hundreds ran for the main tunnel to escape drowning, trampling any guard that stood in their way. Staying clear of the on rush by climbing on a large boulder, I kept my eye on that elevator. Spying a guard on the far side of the on-rush, I made a leap over the tops of the running hordes knocking him to the ground. Gaining my feet again I gave him a boot to the head. From the now unconscious body, I searched for the laser, took it and ran for an out of the way crevice among some rocks to work. After prying the back off the device I proceeded to make some adjustments.

"This thing was obviously preset for a low setting," I said keeping an eye on both the water and the trampling mass. "Let's see if we can't amp it up a little." A wire here, a bypass there. Snapping the cover back in place, I looked up just in time to see a guard on top of me with a laser of his own. "Whoa, test drive!" I aimed the newly adjusted laser in his direction. Both lasers went off. "SNAP!" Just as I felt a sharp pain burst into my shoulder, The laser I was holding lanced out with a red beam burying itself in my opponent's chest and proceeded out the back. The guard fell face down on the ground landing on my boots. "Ok," I said with some satisfaction. "That'll work."

Getting to my feet, I made my way over to the elevator. As I approached, the doors slid open revealing a guard inside. "SNAP!" The laser found it's mark again and another guard fell to the floor. Pushing the dead guard out of the door way the elevator closed. There were three buttons on a small panel the back wall, I hit the first one.

The elevator began to climb and then, unexpectedly twist. The ride was short and the doors opened to reveal a small corridor, which then lead to an observation deck overlooking a colossal room. As I looked out the broad windows of the deck, I stood stunned. There, down on the gigantic floor, looked to be a ship in the early stages of construction, and looking oh so very much like the Star Shark itself.

"Well, well, well," I said a little taken back. I paced back and forth staring in disbelief. The craft, still mostly framework, sat on a series of complex support beams as though waiting for skilled hands to finish the job. "Now I know why they asked me not to come this planet. Had some plans of their own goin'. Although...," I stopped and looked closer at the partially built craft sitting there in the dim light. "This hasn't been touched in awhile, has it? A long while." The place, did indeed, look to have been abandoned some time ago, leaving the ship unfinished and untouched. No one on Maru has the knowledge to help A-Meel build a ship like this. But there was once, wasn't there. Maybe A-Meel wasn't alone in his little venture after all. I stood there with my eyes fixed on the craft caught up in theorizing. First the abandon mine, which Molly and I almost fell to our deaths in, and now this. I certainly have some important questions for the council; like why does the first mine look to have been here long before A-Meel's supposed first visit? And who the heck started building this thing, and why did they just up and abandon it? Then it struck me. "Cause they were here before he was and couldn't find the polynesium either, that's why," I said, slapping the glass.

I turned and headed for the elevator. "Besides," I said with a bit of pride. "They're building the ship all wrong." I pushed the button to call back the elevator and squatted on the floor while aiming my laser. As I waited for the elevator doors to open, I expected the possibility of a guard popping out of it and stood at the ready on the floor. The doors opened, the elevator was empty. "Ok, let's try another one." I pushed the button and the doors closed. The lift moved then stopped at the next floor.

When the doors opened again, noise from the new level hit me like a brick wall. At the end of a short corridor was a room loaded with electronics, computers, power equipment, and similar paraphernalia. In the center of the room was an hour glass shaped column that reached from the ceiling down to a pit of water through a large hole in the floor. Within the column were glowing transparent tubes with wires and circuit boards wrapped and dangling around them on the outside. The whole thing had the appearance of being slapped together at the last minute. "The reactor, I presume," I said being drown out by the noise. "What a nightmare!" I could feel the magnetic radiation vibrating every bone in my body as alarms were going off adding to the din that already flooded the room. Somewhere in the chaos, A-Meel was found racing about to and fro touching controls here and there and failed notice me right away. No guards appeared to be present, only A-Meel alone in a state of panic, rushing about. Entering boldly, I approached one of the control panels and began studying, shaking my head. "Unbelievable! He's totally clueless!"

I looked up and caught A-Meel's glare from across the room. "How's the leg?" I shouted over the clamor.

"You!" He hollered back, bounding over, his face flush with fear and anger. "You did this!" As he came up to push me away from the console I grabbed him by his shirt under his chin and pushed him up against a wall of gages and switches shoving the laser up his nose.

"Yeah, and I'm about to do a lot more! Now where's the off switch? How do we shut this thing down?"

"Shut it down?" he said beginning to stutter. "You can't! There is no way to shut this down!"

"What?! Whaddya mean? Why not?" With my laser still up his nose I drug him over to the column and looked it over closely through the steam that rose from off the water. "You looped it! You've got it in a closed loop! And interrupting the flow just might make it go off! Idiot!" I tightened my grip on his shirt and looked around frantically. "Where's the governor? We might be able to stop it using the governor!"

"What governor? There is no governor!" He said, barely choking a response. "That's what I've been trying to tell you! I need the technology YOU have to...," I gave him a shove to the floor before he could finish.

"You guys are spectacular!" I went back to studying one the control panels, keeping my laser aimed. Spying a length of pipe on the floor, A-Meel slowly began to reach. "How's the leg?" I repeated still focused on the control board. He stopped his hand and retracted it.

I shook my head and threw up my hands. "You built the bloody thing like a fusion reactor! And now it's cascading!"

"I know, you imbecile!" He barked from the floor. "You did that when you blew out the pipes!"

I lost it. Running over and grabbing him by the neck again, I shoved the laser back up his nose. A-Meel's eyes got bigger as he pulled his head back. "No!" I shouted back. "It's been cascading because of your incompetence! You've no idea what yer dealin' with! You can't just throw it together like one of your..., power reactors, or whatever! The only way I can help you with this pile of crap, now, is to lay a bomb on it!" I got up and went over to the pit of steaming water the column stood in. "There's no time." I removed the remaining watch from my wrist and pushed some buttons on it. "I was hoping to tansport back to the ship with this." I threw the watch in the hot caldron. "Forgive me Molly. But there's no way of making it out in time."

"What was that?" A-Meel demanded. "What did you do?" Ignoring him I broke for the elevator only to be met with a painful smack to the leg with the length pipe, causing me to do a face plant to the floor. My adversary wasted no time. In an instant he was on top of me, pipe in hand, doing his best to push it down against my neck. Both of us strained as I did my best to push it and him off of me, but to no avail, he was too heavy. As portly as he had become, I wasn't so sure that I could have done so on a good day, let alone being so tired as I was. "What did you do?" He shouted again. I continued exerting all I could, pushing and straining against his mass but it was definitely a losing battle.

"An..., off..., switch!" I said, barely being able to force the words out between my effort and gritted teeth. "It's on a timer!..., It's..., going to..., explode!" I could feel his strength relaxing a bit as confusion formed on his face. Then it dawned on him.

"Then we will die together!" He said increasing his downward force. While his focus was on my neck, I was able to free my legs and get them up around my rival's own chest. With a single push using any remaining strength I had, I sent him flying to the floor.

"You go ahead," I panted, quickly getting to my feet and running for the elevator. "I've got other plans." I had set the timer on my watch for only a few seconds, before throwing it in, and I was sure those precious few seconds were all but up by now.

"NO! YOU CAN'T! " A-Meel scrambled to his feet and followed me. "WAIT!" The elevator doors almost shut with me standing inside alone, but at the last minute he managed to pry it open again and joined me. The doors closed and the lift began to move. Then all went black.

Miles away Molly stood in the cool evening air looking back toward the direction of the castle that lay somewhere in the forest beyond the hills out of sight from the village. She had finally made her way back home rejoining her family, but did it alone. The stranger came, stole her heart, then left. But, in truth, he was no stranger. For years he had occupied her dreams as she slept, showing her wondrous and magical things that she could not understand or begin explain. And then one day there he was like the fairy tales she heard as a child coming to life. Who would have believed it! She didn't believe it.

"It not fair," Molly thought, "to tease like that. To play with a girl's heart so." Her eyes remained fixed on the tree covered horizon. She thought that maybe if she stared long enough she might see him coming down the road for her.

Then suddenly a low BOOOM shook the ground where she stood as though an earth quake had just ripped its way through the valley. Somewhere beyond the trees, over the hill, thick black smoke rose into the air! BOOOOM a second explosion, and then a third! Molly's eyes grew big as she took a deep breath and held it.

"NEEA!" she screamed, as she burst into tears falling to her knees. "ENCE! NEEA, NEEA!" She put her head to the ground and began to cry uncontrollably.

CHAPTER THIRTEEN

REUNION

"I think he's commin' around Doc."

"Hold real still now, almost got it." I felt something in my left ear. Heard voices. My head throbbed along with some sharp pain in both ears and my left leg was killing me. "Ok, let's check the other one more time." That was Doc! I recognized Doc's voice. A hand turned my head and then something was inserted into my other ear. Blurred images now. I blinked and tried to raise my hand to my eyes.

"Hey Skipper! Welcome back!" That was George! George is here! The thing in my ear went away, then some rattling and scuffing. I made on effort to sit up which made my head throb worse.

"Nice and easy Captain, you've got a serious concussion." Doc's voice again. I felt hands helping me up.

"Hey! How ya feelin' ol' buddy?" George asked.

"Where am I?" I moaned, rubbing eyes again.

"Sick bay. Thought you were a goner there."

"I feel like a goner. What happened?"

"You tell me. All I know is that when the E.M. field finally dissipated we were able to use the scanners again, so we pulled you out of what looked to be an elevator car, all buried in some rubble."

"Yes," I said remembering. "It exploded."

"What did?"

"The reactor. I blew up the reactor." My vision seemed to be clearing. "Where's my glasses?"

"Skipper, you blew up the entire castle." George put the glasses in my hand. "There must've been other things down there too, 'cause there was two secondary explosions after the first one, blew a huge crater where the castle used to be, I mean there is absolutely nuthin' left. You're lucky to be alive man!" Putting my glasses on, I looked around trying to focus. George stood peering at me with my kids behind, all standing there staring with big worried eyes.

"Hi guys!" I called out.

"Hi dad," Melody said in weak uncertain voice. "How ya doin' Dad?"

"I'll be ok," I waved them over, putting my arms around as many as I could at once. "You're Dad is going to be just fine, right Doc?"

Just then The doctor came over and pressed something against my neck. There was a sudden burst of pressure with a "HISSS".

"We missed you, Dad," said Sandy

"Ok, that should help with the pain," The Doc began. "Here's the list. You've had a heavy concussion, two burst ear drums, and your left leg was broken in two places. Now, I've knitted the bones back together, but you're still going to feel some residual pain for a while, that goes with your ears too. And as far as that concussion, I did what I could but you're still going to need rest for a few days."

"George!" I blurted getting caught by a realization. "Was there anybody else in there with me, in the elevator I mean, when you pulled me out?"

He looked puzzled. "No. Just you."

"You're sure?"

"Yeah, no one."

"Whatever that elevator was made out of, it must've protected us." My head still buzzed and throbbed. "At least to some degree."

"Us?"

"A-Meel and myself."

"Who? Anyway, I've got somethin' to show ya." George turned on a monitor close by and drew my attention toward it. "We've found it!"

"What's that?"

"The polynesium!" He exclaimed. That caught my attention for sure. I made an effort to slide off the examination bed to stand up, but found that my equilibrium had other ideas.

"Oooh ouch." Pain crawled up my leg when I put pressure on it, but with the help of my children around me, I managed to limp over to George's monitor for a closer look.

"Look at this!" As George pushed a button on the monitor, my mouth fell open. "Ok, now watch." He pushed the button again and an overlay image fell on top of the first.

"Whoa! Incredible!" I was stunned. "Can you go from an orbital view to a cross section?"

"Sure," said George as he pushed the buttons again. The image changed. Forgetting all about the pain, I was completely captivated.

"I don't believe It. There it is underneath the village the whole time, and loads of it! Enough to cover a whole city! It's Unbelievable!"

"Now you need polynesium to find polynesium," George reminded, "otherwise it will just look like shale rock or something to an ordinary scanner and you'll never find it."

"Maru hid it from him and he couldn't find it." I mumbled to the view screen.

"What?"

"Something our friend Manotu said while we were in that jail cell." The kids helped me back to the bio bed. "Apparently they believe that Maru is alive and this polynesium is the power to which she lives and gives life to the planet. It does appears to be affecting everything about their lives, their health, their ability to heal others and possibly even more that we haven't discovered yet."

"One more thing." George pushes a button again and another layer forms on the last. "This is the village here in this clearing, and these are the other clearings round about."

I got up again to look. "And this?"

George points to the screen. "If you look you'll see that where ever there's polynesium there's no trees, they can't grow there. But instead there's this." He zooms in on the image.

"Herb plants and stuff," I said finishing for him. "Yes, They're fantastic. I had some experience with 'em myself. It's as though the polynesium is having some sort of effect on the plant's growth, effecting it's DNA somehow." Just then a thought struck me as I made myself comfortable on the bed again. "I wonder...,"

"What's that?"

"Well, you remember me telling you about how my dad found some strange and unusual plants when he went diving one day, the same place he found the first polynesium rocks?"

"Yeah. You thinkin' that maybe this is the same plant? Bit of a long shot."

"Yeah, maybe." My mind began to drift. "But ya know funny thing. Mom, when she was alive, would go diving with him on most trips. She was a bit of a botanist of sorts, it seems, loved to go with him and study all the underwater plants and things. She was also a bit of a health nut too. Crazy thing, she'd always try and find edible plants n' stuff for us to eat, so she had this wild idea that maybe some of that sea weed might be good to eat as well. And Dad told me that, when she was pregnant with me, she went down with him, collected a whole bunch of the stuff, and would eat it. Weird. Sometimes she'd come up with some bizarre ideas." Snapping back to the present, I refocused on the monitor. "But, anyway, this place is a gold mine in so many ways." I sat back again. "Such a peaceful people living a simple life in the middle of all of this power. Incredible with you think about it. George, when the word gets out about this place..."

"They won't be able to defend themselves." George said finishing the obvious.

"My wife!" I cried abruptly, shifting my thoughts. "She must think I'm dead!" Suddenly every eye in the room was on me, as in perfect unison they all erupted at once.

"Wife?!?"

"Molly! I've got to find Molly!" I jump off the table and painfully made for the door.

"Now hold it there, Captain!" Piped the Doctor.

"Molly is your wife?" Asked George. "This otta be good. Just what happened down there?"

I popped my head back in room from the corridor. "Set us up for landing, I wanna be on the ground before their sun up." I disappeared then popped my head back in once more. "What time is it down there?"

"Now Captain!" Said the Doctor, trying again.

"About two hours, or so, before their sun up, I think."

"Right. Thanks." I disappeared again leaving the rest looking at each other perplexed.

"Doc, just how bad was that concussion?" George asked. After a quick shower and a change of clothes, into my own uniform, I was on the bridge.

"Count us down, please, Mister Cooper," I was trying to make myself comfortable in my seat amid the list of discomforts I was currently enduring from my leg and head.

"Engaging…, in ten minutes." George called from the helm. "The trajectory should put us right on top of the village."

I pressed a button on the arm of my chair. "All hands this is the captain. Prepare for reentry we're going for a landing."

After a moment the officer at operations, behind me, spoke. "All decks report ready sir." I sat back and let my mind wonder off as I reviewed the last few days and all we had been through.

"Molly," I whispered. "I can't feel my Molly."

"Five minutes to program," George interjected snapping me awake. He turned in his chair. "You sure this is ok? I mean, it's like…well we're gonna land a starship in the middle of a bunch of people from the dark ages."

"No, it's ok," I assured him. "They've been seeing much more from our friends the Pasarins the last few years. Beside we'll be setting it down in the dark and cloaked. Shouldn't draw too much attention." Although I knew in my mind that it would definitely be a rude awakening for many once the ship was seen. My mind drifted again.

"Molly," I whispered again. "Where are you? Why can't I feel you?"

"One minute. How's yer head," George said turning around again.

"I'm ok," I said. George held his gaze at me for a second. "Really, I'm fine." The truth was that I was still feeling more than just a little lightheaded.

"Thirty seconds," he reported. "All decks stand by." He looked over again. "So why are we doin' this again? Landing I mean?"

"Scanners," I commanded trying to act sharp.

"Scanners show clear sir." Piped an officer seated to George's right.

"Inertial dampeners on full."

"Eye sir, inertial dampeners on full."

"Well," I said, "I have a plan…, I think."

"Not going to say?" George turned back to his control board with a sigh. "Ya know I hate it when you do that."

"Secure windows for reentry," I commanded.

"Shunts down and locked," said the operations officer behind me.

"Check the gear."

"Landing gear shows green," said George. He then started the countdown. "Program in five…, four…, three…, two…, one…, Program engaged." The planet on the main view screen began to pitch as the ship moved. "Attitude set, retro's firing." His fingers danced across his control board. "We're go for a cold reentry."

As the ship sliced through the upper atmosphere, I did my best to focus on the task at hand but I kept thinking of Molly. Maybe it was my concussion or perhaps I was too far away now. No because I had dreams of her clear from earth before. Molly, where are you?

My number one man called out the numbers as we quickly descended, cutting our way through Maru's night air. "Twenty thousand now," he announced. "Fifteen thousand, straight down the pipe." Not much else was said as we all appeared to be deep in thought watching the fantastic view unfold before us. "Ten thousand."

"Open the vents," I finally said. "Retract the shunts."

"Vents open," the operations officer responded. "Window shunts retracted."

"Scanners wide open, all clear," said another officer. Even though the landing procedure went very quickly, It still seemed to go on all to long as I was impatient to get down and find out what happened to Molly. Using the T.D.S. to pop down again certainly would have been faster, but I was praying that my plan of actually landing would have the effect that I was hoping for.

"She's closed me out," I mumbled. "Must think I'm dead. She's closed me out completely."

"Two thousand feet," said George. I was wide awake now my eyes going from the main view screen to the ship's scanner.

"Ok, we're looking for their farm house," I told the pilot. "Set us down behind the barn in the goat pasture, behind that group of trees there."

"Front door service, eh? Five hundred feet." George's skill with the large craft was unmatched even to mine, second only to Maxx himself. Faith in his abilities was never a problem, and I could trust him to land it on a cat's whisker if we had to do so. "We're gonna sit awfully large skipper. Those trees aren't gonna be big enough to hide nothin'."

"Not a big deal, I'm not trying to hide it exactly. I have an idea."

"Would be nice to know what that is. Ten feet and…, we seem have a problem."

I jumped up and looked over George's shoulder. "What's the problem?"

The problem was simple, although we failed to consider the possibility occurring, even though we were in fact landing in a pasture. "Goats," answered George.

"Goats? You're kidding." I looked deeper into his control board. "Down viewer." He pushed some buttons. "Ok, problem is they can't see us. Switch to cloak mode two." This mode would make the ship visible to the eye but still remained invisible to scanners, radar, and the like.

"Switching to Mode two." The sudden appearance of large unexplainable mass hovering over the heads of the goats caused them to disperse in all directions rather quickly, hitting the side of the barn, the fence, and then to run out to the far end of the pasture. "All clear," George reported.

"Land this bad boy!"

"Gear going down," George reported touching the controls. "Five feet…, four…, three…, two…," The smooth, sleek, spacecraft, slightly longer than a navy destroyer, sat down ever so gracefully on the soft moist ground. "and…, touch down."

"All stations at keeping," I commanded, getting up and heading for the door. "George You're with me, Mister Brewman, you've got the bridge. And keep yer eye on the sky."

"All stations at keeping, aye sir, I've got the bridge."

George followed me out the door and down the corridor trying to keep up with my impatience. "By the way Skipper," he said finally catching up. "Did we forget about that unknown craft still in orbit?"

"Nope. I've got bigger fish right now." The truth was, that I had figured out what it was already.

As we worked our way down the ship's six decks, I proceeded to give George a quick rundown on my little adventure after he and I got separated. I told him all about A-Meel Me-lot, Molly being kidnapped, our adventure on the run, as well as my discovery of the partially built craft under the castle.

"Sounds like you've been to hell and back. By the way...," He asked eyeing my limp and me rubbing my head. "When are you gonna get some rest like the doctor ordered? How long has it been? And how longs it been since you've eaten?"

"I'm almost there." I pushed the button to open the large circular elevator in front of us. "I promise. You got the a..., who-ha's?"

"Right here," He said patting his shirt pocket. Two sets of large double doors slid open revealing a large circular room which acted as both an airlock and elevator to the ground outside. We stepped in and let the doors close behind us. Pushing a button on the control panel the lift began to lower us outside under the belly of the beast as witnessed by the ship's hull slipping past the two oval windows in the doors.

"Why am I so nervous," I asked, fumbling with my fingers.

"I don't know." George looked at me with a smile. "Why are you nervous?" As the elevator stopped the big doors opened to the chilly, early morning air outside. "Ok, so what's the big plan?" He said as we stepped out into pasture.

"Well, every morning, somebody comes out with buckets to fetch water or somethin'," I said pointing to the house just behind the barn.

"And your bettin' it's gonna be Molly this morning?"

"Yes, but I want her to see me before she sees the ship. This way, she won't be able to see it until she comes closer to me. I'm not sure how she'll take this whole thing though." We walked until we were out from under the ship's belly then George held back as I continued on a little ways further. "Silly, isn't it?"

"No," George said. "I understand what yer tryin' to do. And if I understand what you've told me, it sounds like she's been seein' you in a dream, the whole time you were seeing her, including the Shark. Which I still can't get over, really."

"But don't you see, to have a extraordinary dream then have it suddenly show up on your door step, I mean, how would you take it?"

"I know, that's what I'm saying. This whole thing is absolutely incredible. We could turn around right now if you like, and think of another way."

"No," I said stopping. "This has to be done. I just don't know If I'm doing it right."

I turned around and looked back at the Shark poised in the field. The trees that stood beside it looked so short now. How out of place the ship looked and so menacing silhouetted against the morning sun that just began to peek over the horizon. "I sure hope I don't wind up scaring the willies out of her."

"Skipper!" Whispered George as he pointed and nodded back toward the house. I turned to look and beheld Molly carrying two metal buckets from around one side of the house. My heart began to pound in anticipation of what was about to take place. I watched her for a moment as she looked to be headed toward the well on the other side. And then I made a familiar sound, "puttttth." She stopped and glanced over to where the sound came from, then froze. The buckets she was carrying dropped from her fingers and clattered on the ground.

Screaming, she picked up her skirt and began running toward me, bawling. I stood where I was, on the other side of the fence, and waited for her approach. "ENCE!" she shrieked! I couldn't seem to hold back my own emotions, with tears beginning to fill my own eyes now. "ENCE!" she wailed again as she climbed over the fence and into the goat pasture.

She came within five feet of me and then suddenly froze, her eyes becoming fixed on the gigantic, indescribable monster that was resting in the pasture with us, reflecting the early morning sun. The Star Shark sat with majestic repose as if it were a sleeping beast from another era, an enormous bird that had somehow taken refuge among her goats. Her face went blank as her mouth gaped as she first looked at the ship then at me, then at the ship again, then at me. Slowly Molly began to collect her reason as she came up to me and very gently touched my glasses, then moved her hand down to my uniform examining it closely, with another glance over at the mammoth metal beast spread out behind us.

"Rock n' roll," I said softly putting on a big smile. I could see the fight going on in her mind as she wrestled with the idea of a dream actually coming to life in front of her. The proof had literally landed right at her own door step. And yet she had entrusted her heart and her life to me long before this moment, not completely understanding just who or what I am. Then again, maybe our special connection had been giving her more insight than I was aware.

"Ence?" She asked finally though her tears.

"Yes, eea," My arms slowly found their way around my new wife. "It's me." Grabbing me tight, I put my arms around her, picked her up, and swung her around. "YES!" I hollered out in jubilee. I then put my face to hers. "Hello."

"Good morning," she replied, her face beaming as I then gave her a proper hello with a kiss. George walked up to us from where he was standing clearing his throat. Molly and I stood steadfast, still linked, as George cleared his throat a few more times.

"We've got guests," he said nodding toward the house. Looking up I could see Mama, Kerry, and two little boys, who looked to be about five and ten years old, approaching. Each, as they drew nearer, went through the same shock and awe as the Star Shark came within their view.

Molly hollered something at them waving them over. After a few moments their fear of whatever that thing was in the pasture, waned a little and they did as Molly bade, their mouths scooping up the same ground.

"Um, Skipper," George pointed to another direction.

"Oh my," I became a little shocked, as most of the towns folk appeared to be gathering together a few thousand yards outside the pasture. The astonishing spectacle, that I had provided, seemed to be drawing more attention than we have first thought. But while the fascination drew them in, trepidation on just what was happening held them back, at least for now.

Meanwhile Mama and Kerry had climbed over the fence to join us, their mouths still open.

"George," I held my hand out to him while still holding on to Molly with the other one. "If I may." He reached into his shirt pocket, pulled out a small device and placed it in my hand.

"Hello George," Molly said with a big smile.

"Well, hello yerself little lady," replied George with a bit of surprise. "Teachin' her a bit of English I see."

"Looks kinda like blue tooth for a cell phone," I said looking the small device over.

"It's fairly complete. It will continue to update and correct itself as it hears more. It's also connected to the ships com system."

"Alright. Good job." I placed it in my left ear. Molly watched with curiosity on her face. I held my hand out again as George then gave me another. "Ok, now, don't say nothin'," I told him as I pushed back Molly's hair and placed the second in her left ear. The last time I reached in her ear I pulled out a gold coin. This time I was about to give her a lot more.

I reached up to my ear piece and pushed a small button causing it to give off a "Beep" in my ear. I then pushed the button on Molly's, when hearing the "beep" she gave me a surprised look. Taking her face in my hands I spoke to her again. "Good morning beautiful lady." Confusion covered Molly's face as she put a hand to her left ear. I continued. "I am so very sorry for leaving you as I did. I had to save your people and was afraid you'd get hurt."

"Yane ohna pasee ta," She piped, a little shocked. "You do not speak in my tongue and yet..., I hear you?" The translator was working perfectly. "How can this be? What magic is this?"

"No magic."

"You understand my words?" Complete surprise still filled her face as she looked to her mother and then to me. "There is so much I have wanted to say, but..., How is it happening?"

"How's it workin'? George asked.

"Yes, great, I understand everything." I was still looking Molly.

"Whats happening?" I could hear Mama ask.

"What are they doing? Added Kerry.

"M'ma! I hear him!" Molly's surprise had turned to elation. "I understand him! He can understand me!" She turned to me again. "My People owe you a great dept. We cannot repay you for what you have done."

"Ah shucks, twas nothin'," I chuckled. "You've already repaid me, with more than I could ever ask for." Her face went flush. I would love to think this was all over but I knew in my heart that it wasn't. A-Meel Me-lot was still out there somewhere. "George, may I barrow yours for a minute? I wanna talk to Mama."

"Sure." He put it in my hand and I walked over to her. Very gently I put the translator in her ear as she stood there frozen unsure of what was about to happen next.

"It's ok M'ma," I heard Molly say. "He wants to talk to you."

"What?" She asked still frozen. I took her hand in mine.

"I want to thank you for the generosity and kindness you've shown us." I told her.

"Oh." she said with a shock as she looked at me then Molly.

"When I saw you, I then knew where your daughter got her beauty." I then kissed her on the cheek.

"Oh…, well…, grace be to you, and you are very welcome," she forced a smile through her nervousness. "Can he understand me?"

"Yes M'ma." Molly turned to me again. "I suppose you are going to leave us now, go back to the stars in your sky boat."

"No!" I shook my head. "Oh no, my beautiful lady. Never! Maru is my home now, that is if you'll have me. Are we not claimed now? Besides, somebody has to protect you, and this wonderful people."

"We are…, claimed," she said with some hesitation. "I was not sure you were bound by our laws." She looked at the ground. "If you really wanted…, wanted to stay with me…, I mean. I thought maybe…" Before she could say anything more I scooped her in my arms and kissed her.

"People are watching," she whispered.

"Really?" I asked laughing, kissing her again.

"Please, put me down," Molly begged smiling, her face flush.

"Well, is it not the custom for a man that has been claimed, to provide a home for his new family?" I asked.

"Well, yes but…"

"Well," I said turning toward my ship. "Welcome home." Then I noticed them. "Molly look." I pointed at the ship. "See? In the windows? They're waving."

"Waving?"

"Yeah, up there, in the windows right there. See 'em?"

"There is somebody up there," she said finally noticing.

"Yeah, those are my children."

"You have children?" She asked giving me a different look than before.

"Yes."

"You are their P'pa? Is there M'ma their too?"

"No. No mother. Just me." As I walked toward the ship's entryway with Molly in my arms, her look kept changing as she attempted to sort that one out. "It's also an Earth custom for a man to carry his new bride over the thresh hold of their new home."

"It is?"

"It is."

"In there?"

"Sure why not?" I stepped into the lift that was still poking down from the ship's belly. "A…, George, I'm going to go a…, show her the a…, ship."

"Don't worry about me," said George with a big smile, "knock yerself out, I'm going to go fraternize."

"You ready?" I asked Molly.

"I…, a…," The doors closed and began to lift us up in to the ship. "OH!" Startled, Molly grabbed on to me tight.

Our first stop was sick-bay to give Molly a quick check. I knew she was a lot healthier than me, by far, but I had another reason on my mind for taking her there first. Then it would be to finally put some real food in my stomach and to get some much needed rest, either of which I hadn't had in a couple of days.

As we traversed through the ship, Molly's eyes were as big a saucers trying to take in all the magic that was around her. It would certainly take a while for any of it to make any kind of sense to her, but time was what we now had.

"Hey Doc." I walked in the sick bay, Molly in hand. The first thing that seemed to captivate her was the doors that slid open all by themselves. I pulled on her hand as she seemed to have her eyes stuck on the crack trying to see just where the door went.

"Doc, this is Molly. Molly, this is Doc. He a physician. He just wants to take a look at you, make sure everything is ok."

"Ooya na," said Doc greeting her with a smile.

"Ooya na." She said slowly her eyes now fixed on the walls of blinking lights especially the big light on the ceiling illuminating the room. "How does it do that?"

"Sit right up here sweet heart," I said patting the bio bed. "Just a quick peek at yer insides."

"My insides?"

Doc waved a pocket scanner up and down her, with another hand pushing buttons on a control panel beside him. He then began to focusing intently on her head.

"Fascinating." He then moved down to her stomach. "Well, well," He chuckled. "This is interesting. I guess congratulations is in order."

"What is it?" I went over and glanced at the image the scanner had found. Giving the scanner back to the doctor I put my hand on Molly's stomach, a big smile dressing my face.

"What is it?" She said worried.

"Well, right now it pretty small, but, in about nine months it will be something indeed…, Mama." Her face lit up, her own hand covering her stomach now.

"Really? Me?"

"Umm Captain." Doc put the scanner down. "I need you to come back later. After scanning this lady here, I think I found something that will intrigue you."

"What's that?"

"Well, I'm going to run some tests to make sure, but I think I found an answer to one of your biggest questions."

"I'll be down in a few hours or so and will take a look then."

"I going to be M'ma!" Molly glowed with the thought it.

"And Molly, make sure he gets some rest now, ya hear?" ordered Doc. "He needs it."

We left sick-bay and began to make our way to the upper decks. "I'm going to be M'ma." She repeated, a smile covering her face. "He called you…, captain. What is…, captain?" Molly asked still distracted by what was around her.

"I built the ship and I command it. I am the leader here."

"You are Lord here? Lord of the sky boat? All of this is yours?"

"Yeah, you could say that." I held her hand tight as we walked. "Molly, I have so much I want to show you. There are so many wonderful things out there that I am just so excited to show you."

"Things are happening so fast for me," She said shaking her head as if to shake away all the confusion and sort it all out. "I barely know where I am, and what's happening."

Minutes later we finally arrived at my quarters, her eyes grew as big as ever as she looked around. "This is yours?"

"This is my cabin. This is where I spend most my personal time. And now your cabin too." The main entrance opened up to a large comfortable sitting room. Two semi circular couches sat in front of large angled windows that lined one wall with a collection of easy chairs on either side, complete with two glass coffee tables. Against another wall, two glass lamps sat on two wood desk tables with a single over sized flat panel monitor on the wall above them. Pictures and paintings hung on the walls here and there. "And over here…" I walked her over to a doorway. "Is my private galley. Which is another name for a ship's kitchen."

"It's huge! This cabin is bigger than my house. Where is the hearth?"

"And over here, in this room," I continued to lead her. "Is where I sleep, and just beyond is where I wash my clothes and take a bath."

She was shaking her head again. "This is too much. It's like a palace. This whole thing is like a palace, and so many magical things." She turned to me in bewilderment. "I don't think I can do this, I don't understand anything. I don't deserve any this!"

I took her and sat her down on the bed with me still holding her hand tight. "Oh yes you do." I kissed her. "You are the most wonderful lady in whole universe. And if I remember the dreams I've been having, and am able to make sense of them, you been through a lot more than you've told anybody."

"Dreams? You've had dreams of me? I've had dreams, but could not make sense of them. No one would help me. People just laughed and told me I was sick."

"Well, here I am, sitting here among your..., goats, or whatever they are. What do they say now? At night I would dream of you, of your family, and of this world that you live. These dreams have been coming to me for a very long time, right here in this bed." I watched her as she sat quiet for a moment lost in thought. "And now, here you are! I can hardly believe it myself! Maybe I'm still in a dream right now." I kissed her on the hand as she continued to look around. "One day at a time. Let's just take it one day at a time."

"Just in the last moments you've shown me more than I have ever thought possible." Her mind still seemed to be losted in a fog.

"Do you realize just how wonderful this has been to just sit here, like this, and be able to actually talk with you?"

"Yes, but..., WOW!" She gave me a big smile. "This has been so..., wonderful and...,a little frightening, if you can imagine. I guess I should just be calm, and as you say, one day at a time. There is so much for me to learn, but I need not learn it all at once."

"Speaking of being calm," I stretched out flat on the large king sized bed and let out a big sigh. "Time for some much needed sleep. Oh this bed feels good."

"There will be a union feast tonight in my village to celebrate those who have been recently claimed now." Molly stood up giving me some foot room.

"You wanna go?"

"We have been claimed and will now be part of the feast to celebrate." She began to remove my shoes and socks. "M'ma will be preparing food with the others..., for us."

"Oh yes, of course. Did you want to go and help her?"

"I do," she smiled. "But I will stay with my husband now, and help him sleep." Molly appeared to be accepting her situation a little better than I had hoped, which is remarkable considering the new world that I have thrust her into. But I knew, that over time, she would continue to relax, when she began to understood more. I found her to be a very smart lady, and even though she feels a few steps out of pace, her ability to adapt appears to be quite remarkable. She reached behind her neck and began unbuttoning her dress, which eventually fell to the floor.

CHAPTER FOURTEEN

THE SECRET

I turned over to my left side and threw my arm over..., oops no Molly! Opening my eyes and sitting up I looked around. She was no longer in bed with me or in the room either. If she had wondered off somewhere she may have gotten lost or even hurt and I would never forgive myself. I was just about to dart out of bed and start a search, when the door slid open and in dashed Molly in an obvious state of panic. She had been running to and fro, from one room to another, appearing to be looking for something, desperately. Her face was red, and her hands were holding herself down low, as she scurried about. Then it dawned on me.

"Molly this way!" I said as I went into the bathroom. "I am so sorry. I should have shown you this before we slept. Forgive me." After a very brief introduction to indoor plumbing as well as a quick training on it operation, Molly finally found her relief. "Forgive me." I watched her breath out and slowly melt on the toilet. "How long have you been holding that?" She said nothing but gave me a look that said, "dare you ask?" "No, no, wait. Don't get up yet." I pointed to a small collection of buttons on the wall. "There's no paper..., or corn cobs, leaves, or whatever. When you're finished, before you stand up, push this button right here." She reached over cautiously and placed a finger where I indicated.

"OH!" Molly yelped, almost leaping from the bowl.

"When the sound stops, it's done," I said, holding a laugh down. Then waited for a moment. "All done?"

She nodded, her eyes still big and a hand covering her mouth. When the surprise attack from down below stopped Molly slowly and very cautiously rose. "Anything else you should be telling me?" She asked with a smart look in her eye.

"Well," I said, "We should shower and get dressed for the feast. I'm absolutely dying for a shower."

"Shower?"

"It's like a bath, only quicker and cleaner." Then whispering in her ear, "And lots of fun when you do it with someone."

After the shower came the introduction to important things like deodorant, feminine napkins, underpants, a bra, and the like, things that never would have occurred to me I would have to introduce to anyone. I reached over to my bed stand and pushed a button on the vid-com. "Nanny, would you come in here please?"

"Yes sir, right away sir." The response came in a thick Scottish brogue. The voice was that of a short stocky woman that appeared to be in her mid sixties. She came in presenting herself in an outfit typically suited for a maid. And yes, she was a hologram. Which reminds me. Introducing the existence of holograms may be an adventure in itself but, One thing at a time.

"Nanny, this is Molly."

"Yes sir, congratulations sir." She went over to a half dressed Molly and gave her a hug. "Ooya_na darling,"

"Ooya_na," Molly responded a little taken aback.

"Nanny, Molly and I are going to the union feast tonight and I was wondering if you would help her find something appropriate to wear."

"Oh, yes sir. It would be my pleasure. I think we can replicate somthin' for her quite nice."

"Oh and, show her how to use a bit of makeup and help her with her hair and stuff like that."

"Oh, it'll be no trouble a-tall."

I gathered up the rest of my clothes. "Not that she needs it any of it. She gorgeous just as she is. You guys can do yer thing in here and I'll go dress out there."

"She's beautiful sir," Nanny sang out with a big smile. "We'll get her fixed up right smartly sir. Off ya go then."

With clothes in hand, I went out and into the sitting room and finished dressing, then waited for the girls.

"George?" I called, pressing the vid-com.

"Yes sir."

"Where are ya? How's it goin."

"Doin' fine. I'm down here by the house. Got a little surprise for ya when yer ready to come out. I'm assuming your goin to this union feast thing?"

"Yeah, Molly's gonna be ready here in a moment and We'll be right out, probably in the next few minutes."

"No sweat. You get any sleep?"

"Yeah, some. I'm as hungry as a bear though."

"That's good, cause man, these folks got an awesome feast prepared." Just then the door the bedroom opened. Molly walked out with Nanny just behind.

"Whoa..., looks like they're ready George, I'll see ya..., in just a few..., minutes."

"Roger that. Out."

I stood up from the couch stunned. She was a vision to behold. I had always considered Molly to be one of the most beautiful in the village, but, now…, words could not describe. She had on a full length gown, white with tatted lace here and there, complete with white gloves to the elbows, straight out of a story book fairy tale. Her hair was perfectly done, make up in just the right way. Then it dawned on me, a computer helped do this? Once again Maxx proved himself to be more then he was made out to be. Nanny beamed as she caught my reaction to her finished project. Molly stood there glowing like an angel, a shy look on her face, not knowing what I was would think of her new look.

I got down on one knee and gazed at the ground. "A thousand pardons princess," I began. "I was looking for my Molly. Have you seen her?" Nanny gave a little laugh.

Molly giggled nervously. "You make me cry and you'll ruin my face paint."

"Make up Darlin'," Corrected Nanny as she touched up Molly's eyes.

"You are so beautiful," I whispered. "Wow."

"Thanks," came a quiet response. As I held out my elbow for her, she took it and we went our way.

"Have a jolly time sir," sang Nanny.

*   *   *   *   *   *

As we walked off the ship from the lift into the evening sun, George stood waiting for us by Mama's horse and cart, which had been carefully decorated with strings of flowers that had been laid all over it. Mama, who was also close at hand, came up and gave her daughter a hug, as did Mary and Kerry who stood waiting with their mother. The four of them started their wild chatting and tittering as they awed over Molly's new dress and make up, as well as all the fascinating and magical things Molly had experienced on board the ship from the sky.

"Hey, hey! There they are!" George called out, greeting us with his usual smiling face. Then he caught a look at Molly. "Wow! Gorgeous!"

"Oh my," I laughed noticing the cart. "It's beautiful. I love it."

"I was gonna tie some tin cans on the back, but I guess they invented those yet."

"it's just fine the way it is, George, absolutely beautiful!"

After taking a few moments to relay to her family the adventure of a life time that she was having, she came to me with her hand as I then helped her up on the cart.

"You a…," I gestured toward Mary and Kerry, "doin' yer own socializing?"

A smirk grew on George's face. "If I am, I'll never tell."

"George," I then whispered, "have security at the ready."

"You expecting a guest?"

"I'd be sorely disappointed if he didn't show."

"What makes you think he's even alive?" asked George as I jumped up taking my place beside Molly.

"Oh he's alive, alright. You can trust me on that one. Tell the kids they can come. There's gonna be a lot of young people their age here and there, n' fun stuff to do, but I want them pulled out at the first sign of trouble."

"No problem."

"By the way," I added, glancing around, "Any more of them guards skulking around?"

"Not a chance. After you freed all those guys from the mines, and they figured A-Meel was dead, they took care of business in very short order, rounding all the buggers up. Not that there was very many of 'em left, anyway."

"What happened to 'em?"

"Most went back to their families. The rest are waiting judgment at the Hall of Elders."

"Wow, forgiving bunch aren't they?"

"Oh, don't kid yerself. All of 'em have a penalty of some sort commin', painfully so. Well, have a good time. I'll be there shortly," commanded George waving.

"Yick, yick." Molly gave the rains a jerk.

In just moments we arrived at a large grassy area that had been decked out with candle lamps, strung between tree and post. Flowers ornamented the many round tables that filled most of the lawn, along with larger tables on the outside which presented every kind of fair available. Food was everywhere, as well as questionable drink in large clay jugs. Music came from three to four men, on a small wooden platform, each playing some sort of stringed instrument or flute. It sounded like a combination of old Celtic music, blended with Chinese, with a bit of hillbilly thrown in together, but festive it was, setting the mode for an important occasion.

As we walked in, joining the masses that had already gathered, Molly was greeted by many. There was the usual hugs and tittering as they each in turn looked her over marveling at her new appearance. A few came up to me but, most seemed to stay clear, no doubt out of circumspection. Who is this stranger from the sky anyway, and why has he bonded with one of our own? Is he the one that saved all the men from the mines? Little did they know, that while I wore this small marvel of technology in my ear, I could understand every word quite clearly.

Soon, Molly and I were lead to a table close by the other couples being honored today by the feast. Being as famished as I was, I found little trouble stuffing myself most eagerly as the food was brought. No sooner did I finish one dish then another was quickly presented. I figured this was either an attempt to add a few hundred pounds to my weight or a devious plot to my eventual over throw.

As the tables were all filled with many enjoying the cuisine, many more also danced to the music. Revelry and merriment filled the air as there was no doubt that they were also celebrating their freedom from the oppression that had held them for so long. Five processions of about twenty or more each danced in a circular arrangement, round and round, then back the other way again keeping beat to the song. Jumping up, Molly grabbed me and I soon found myself joining one of the formations. Round and round, then back again, we danced. I've never felt more free, more peaceful then at this moment.

Then suddenly, starting from the back, a stillness began to settle in among the crowd. A scream was heard, and then another. Soon the silence caught all, as eventually, the dancing stopped then the music. The crowd quickly separated allowing a single figure to slowly emerge dragging one leg as he worked his way forward. Stopping, the individual then stood alone in the center of the gathering. "A-Meel," I whispered. He appeared partially burned, battered, bruised, dirty, bleeding, and what clothes he still had on were torn. I signaled George, who was standing not far off, who in turn, signaled the security personnel he had brought with him. Three came over carrying disrupter rifles and aimed them at A-Meel.

"So," I said to him, "How are things?"

A-Meel began to chuckle, then laugh, then laugh loudly.

"It wasn't that funny," I said watching him to walk closer as he continued to laugh, dragging his wounded leg. As he stood in front of me the laughing stopped and turned to anger.

"You can joke if you wish, Captain, but it will be me that will be having the last laugh." I began to feel a little uneasy. "You see, my friend, somewhere in the village, over there," he said pointing. "Is a bomb. A bomb made from my last bit of the mineral you call polynesium." The laughing started once more as I found myself totally aghast! While any bomb, being enhanced with polynesium, would certainly do more damage than one could imagine, essentially eliminating any evidence of the village completely, and much as the forest around, A-Meel had no way of knowing about the city sized load of the stuff which sat directly underneath the village! With that, there were also other clearings caused by this special mineral which would also ignite creating a continent sized crater on one side of the planet.

I walked up to him grabbing what was left of his collar, stunned at what I just heard. "Where is it!"

"You and your technology," he laughed mockingly. "Look for it yourself. And you'd better do it soon."

"Where is it!" I tightened my grip. "Tell me or I'll kill you right here!"

"DO IT!" He shouted, choking through his narrowing collar. "We are a hundred years more advanced than your…, Earth." A-Meel was now having trouble breathing. "And here you come with your new discovery just to show some boasting. If we can't have it, neither can you!" I doubled up a fist and pasted him one as hard as I could on his blacken face, knocking him to the ground. He only lay there laughing harder.

"George!" My anger was now turning to panic. "Call the ship, have 'em scan for that bomb, everywhere! Shouldn't be hard to find!"

"I wouldn't do that!" A-Meel said with a sore, gravelly voice still laughing and coughing, rubbing his throat.

"HOLD THAT!" I yelled back at George. I then bent down to A-Meel still on the ground. "And why not?"

"It has a sensor." He coughed still rubbing his throat. "A sensor that will detect…," He coughed again. "Your scanner…, it will set it off." I was so angry I didn't know what to say next except to get my fist ready for another volley. "It also has a photo-static trigger," A-Meel continued though more coughing. "It's set to go off at first light."

Once again I felt my rage burn within me as I grabbed his hair.

"Let's see how you fair without your precious technology," he added.

I then began to pound on his face as blood began to spurt from his nose.

"ENCE!" Molly screamed running up and holding me back. Then in a calm voice, "No Ence. It's not our way."

I made an effort to collect myself, at least for a moment, shaking my sore knuckles, then stood up and motioned to the three security still standing close by with rifles in hand. "Take him on board and lock him up." As they picked him up and began to drag him off he continued his laughing. "He's mad," I said visibly shaken, as George came walking up. "He's totally out of his mind."

"Well, It's not like we can just load everybody in the Shark and take off."

"No, that would be impossible." I turned to Molly who had a look of terror on her face. "But we had better move fast. How long have we got?"

George put a hand on my shoulder. "It should be dawn in about five hours."

I breathed for a moment trying to clear my mind. "George, first of all, have the ship shut down ALL the scanners! All of them! Completely! Even the hand helds!"

"Got it."

"Molly, I'm assuming you're the only one here, besides George and I, that understood what A-Meel was saying?" I said taping the translator in my ear.

"What is 'bomb'?" She asked with her face still white.

"It's a device. A device that will kill your people..., everywhere, the whole village at once. All at one time. And he has hidden it somewhere in your village." She thought for a minute on the marvel of it all! The horror! The fact that someone had the ability to wipe out a whole village, without an army of soldiers or conventional weapons at all!

"He can do this?! Why would he do this?!"

"Yes..., yes he can, and because he's a very jealous and power hungry man. Please listen carefully pretty lady, here's what I need you to do." I then instructed her not to reveal to her people about the bomb or what it could do, the knowledge of which would certainly cause unwanted panic, but instead, have them help her search for a strange device that would be hidden somewhere in the village. They were instructed not to touch it but to notify me immediately if they found something. With enough of the local men recruited, we began a systematic search, building by building, house by house, street by street, every fruit crate, every barrel, every box, and every tree and bush.

Two hours later I touched my ear piece. "Molly, have you found anything yet?" There was a short pause, as I wondered if Molly would remember how to push the button on her translator as I had showed her.

"No, we have found nothing yet," she finally said.

"Where are you?"

"We are at the church now."

"Oh man," I sighed turning to George "They're moving way too slowly. Maybe I should have went ahead and told them what was at stake, may have moved them a little faster."

"Where are they?" He asked.

"There not even half way yet, and we've been at it for hours. Have you checked through all of that stuff?"

"Yeah," George said. "Everything."

"All right. It's like lookin' for a needle in a hay stack, AND in the dark." I stepped out of a cellar and back outside. "Let's move on the next house. It's beginning to feel like a awfully big village, man."

"They're doin' the best they can."

"Yeah I know." Working around chickens and over fences we headed to the next dwelling. "How long till first light?"

George checked his watch. "I would guess…, should be in about three hours or less."

"Oh crap," I mumbled. "Doin' this in the dark ain't helping none either. Suddenly, I stopped in my tracks. "Wait a minute. We're goin' about this all wrong."

"Why?"

"First light…, he said the bomb would go off at first light." I looked at George. "He put it where it would get light. He said it had a photo-static trigger, remember? What the heck are we doin'?"

"You mean, while we've been wastin' time lookin' around in peoples basements, we could be missing it?"

"I'm thinking it has to be outside somewhere. We should change our search pattern a little bit and start lookin more around out in the yards and fields and stuff."

George shook his head. "We're gonna miss a lot of places that it may be, doin' it that way."

"We just haven't got the time to do it any other way, besides it makes perfect sence." I pressed my ear piece again. "Molly?"

"Ence?"

"Change the way you're searching a little bit. Get out of the cellars and start looking around outside in places. Places that will see the sun when it comes up. That should help speed things up a bit."

"We will…," said the ear piece again. "Ence?"

"Yes?"

"I love you!"

A lump formed in my throat. "I love you too, beautiful lady. Don't worry, we'll find it."

"I know we will."

"That's quite the lady you have there, Vince," George said as we continued to turn over boxes and other objects, flash lights in hand. "You had to go to a completely different planet to find her, but she's a jewel."

"Yes she is. That she is indeed." We continued our frantic search working around porches, out houses, and rain barrels, and the like and moved quickly to the next abode.

More time had passed, and I was beginning to think that the race we were in was a futile one, but the search went on, turning over this, looking behind that, scaring the horses, scattering the goats, and the chickens all over who knows where.

I looked up at George who had paused for a moment and was looking out at the horizon. I looked over with him and saw that the sky was beginning to lighten.

"We're not going to make it, are we?" I mumbled.

"A..., Skipper?" George asked.

"Yeah?"

"Was A-Meel a religious man?"

Odd question I thought. "No," I answered. "Not at all. In fact he seemed have an extreme abhorrence for people who..." I looked at George who was now looking in the other direction. I turned to see what he had found. The tallest point in the village was now beginning to show. It was the church! I looked at George as my heart began to pound. We immediately started on a mad run as I touched my ear piece. "MOLLY! GET EVERYBODY AWAY FROM THE CHURCH! NOW!"

"We are. We're passed the market now," Said my ear piece. "What is it?"

"Get everybody outta there! Go as far as you can!" In the end I knew that even that wouldn't be enough for them.

George and I raced, down the dirt road for the small church as time seemed to be against us the whole way. Looking up occasionally I noticed the steeple getting brighter and brighter the closer we came. As we finally made it to the small structure and went inside, both of us with our lungs heaving, we were startled to see that quite a few folks had gathered inside as all eyes were now on us. Somehow, they had sensed the overwhelming doom wrapping around them and perhaps came in for some consolation.

"George. The steeple!"

"There!" He yelled pointing. The sun was almost up as evidenced from the amount of light coming through the windows. It was only a matter of minutes or even down to seconds now. Racing for the ladder I made it up first as George followed. The hatch to the bell tower was small and the tower cramped, but there in front of us, beginning to catch the first light of the morning underneath the bell, was the bomb!

"No way to disarm it?" George panicked.

"No time," I said pointing out toward the horizon. "Sit over there and block the sun, I have an idea. I took my new watch off my wrist, pushed some buttons then clamped the watch's magnetic bottom to the bomb's metal casing.

"Shark this is the Captain," I said hollering at it.

"Yes Captain."

"Listen carefully. Without using the scanners for a lock conformation, lock the T.D.S. on to my communicator signal, and send it one hundred miles straight up, I repeat..., without using the scanners! Do you have that?"

"Yes sir, but it's your signal sir!"

"Just do it! And do it NOW!" After a short moment the watch and bomb glowed brightly, then vanished. George and I sat there holding our breath for a moment as we stopped to listen. Suddenly, a bright flash split the early morning sky, then slowly faded.

"There it goes, rock n' roll." I sat back and tried to calm my breathing down. "I could still use a good night sleep." I pressed my ear piece, "Molly, we did it. Your people are safe..., the bomb is gone." I then sat back and closed my eyes and breathed out slowly.

"Grace to you! Grace to you!..., He has done it, my people! We are freed once again!" As Molly kept her ear piece button pressed I could hear the people in the back ground cheering. "You've made some friends here my husband!"

"I could hear 'em all cheering in the background," I said to George. "You get the feeling she's told 'em what the scoop was anyway?"

"Well, how's it feel to be the hero?" George sat crouching on the other side of the bell. "At least you didn't have to get wet this time." That started both of us laughing.

"No, I'm no hero," I said, trying to find the energy to stand up again. "Couldn't have done it without you..., or Molly for that matter. You're all heroes." Finding the hole again, I began to climb back down the steeple. "Well, next stop, Pasaris."

"Uh oh," George followed me down. "Is this where the real fireworks start?"

"We'll see."

About an hour later George and I were back at in Mama's goat pasture watching Molly give her Mama and sisters a hug good bye. A huge throng had assembled around us as everything from handshakes to hugs to pats on the back seemed to be completely unavoidable. I was never very comfortable in accepting the role of the hero, not to mention being center stage in a large crowd and found myself looking forward to getting underway as soon as possible, back into the comfortable surroundings that the emptiness of space offered. But somehow that wall, that both George and Maxx said that I had put around myself, felt as though it was finally coming down, or at least a little bit. Perhaps it was due to the incredible peace that I found here, or the unpretentious life these people had created for themselves. But, whatever the reason, I would consider Maru my home now, and I would find my heart permanently anchored in this peaceful world.

I went up to Mama and took my turn for the next hug, as George seemed to be making a rather lengthy good by to a certain brunet. "We will return," I told Mama. She being without the little ear piece Molly did the translating this time. "You are a very special people, and I love you all." I then kissed her.

Moments later Molly and I were back on board the Star Shark. I had chosen a very special room for Molly's first flight, opening up a world of wonder, that would only be the beginning of an unbelievable and magical journey, beyond any dream she may have had before. For this I brought her to the ship's large, main dining hall which had huge panoramic windows that wrapped around the front and sides, providing a breathtaking view to any who came in.

"Wow," she whispered, as she cautiously walked in, now viewing the scene outside from several stories up. From her new vantage point, she could see the huge crowd that had gathered just outside the ship, and now almost her whole village.

I took her across the room and right up against the front expanse of windows for the best view in the house, then raised my watch to my face. "Take us up George. Give us a couple of orbits before setting course for Pasaris."

"You got it," my watch responded.

"Hold on to your corsets," I said holding on to Molly's hand. The ship's wings, once again, flashed their strobes as witnessed by the concourse of villagers gathered on the ground who then began to back away, making room for the enormous craft that had landed in their village.

Ever so gently the ground began to drop away. Molly's knees buckled slightly as she spread her arms out grabbing on to me tightly as if to steady herself, to keep from falling off into the great wide open that suddenly spread out before her. Artificial gravity and as well as the inertial dampeners kept anyone aboard from feeling any movement what so ever, but the amazement of the event now taking place was one of almost shock for this first time rider of the skies.

As the ground began to move past us at greater and greater speeds, I then found her on all fours, astonishment dressing her face as she became frozen to the floor being afraid to move even an inch. I got down with her on my stomach leaning on my elbows watching the spectacle unfold out the large windows. "Wow!" I whispered. Molly gave a brief nervous giggle but remained petrified. "Molly, Look!" I pointed out the window. "That's where the castle was, that big hole there." A gigantic crater filled with water from the nearby river now lay where the majestic age old castle once stood. Very little of the structure remained to give evidence of the evil that took place there. "That must've been one fantastic explosion, Thanks for the look George," I said to my watch.

"I figured you'd like to see what it looked like," It said back to me. "It's a complete miracle you're still alive, ol' buddy."

Soon the ground dropped lower and lower as our ship climbed into Maru's upper atmosphere. A thick haze slowly covered the ground as mountain tops pushed their peaks upward, reaching past the layers of clouds that drifted even higher.

Molly laid on her stomach with me now, relaxing a little, but still holding on to me as tight as she could, witnessing for the first time a vision that will instill itself within her forever.

The sky grew darker and darker slowly revealing the uncountable stars that literally blanketed the heavens, as the planet gradually gave evidence to its roundness, displaying its indescribable beauty to the very few who had ever ventured this far.

"It's so..., beautiful," She said, finally speaking. "I had no idea. We won't fall?" I reached over and kissed her cheek.

"No, we won't fall," I reassured her. "No matter how many times I see this sight, I never get tired of it. There's simply no way to describe it. You have to see it for yourself to believe."

She then turned to look at me as a new light had lit in her eyes. "I understand now! I understand what you were trying to tell me with the rocks and the rocano fruit."

"You mean the stink oranges?" I asked.

Molly laughed. "Yes, the stinky rocanos. This is so beautiful! I remember seeing all of this in my dreams, but I did not understand what I was seeing. But now..., I think I begin to understand."

"Once you have tasted flight, you will forever walk the earth with your eyes turned skyward, for there you have been, and there you will always long to return." I had my arm around her, holding her softness next to me. "An earth man named Leonardo da Vinci once said that a very long time ago."

"He sounds like he was a very wise man."

"You know somethin'?" I asked.

"What"

"I've never felt happier then right now."

"Ah." She kissed me, and then kiss me again.

"Whatcha doin' Dad?" Melody asked interrupting a moment. I was suddenly aware that all of my kids were gathering around laying on the floor with us.

"How come your on the floor?" Sandy asked.

"Hey guys!" I called gathering a couple of 'em up next to me. "Where ya been hidin'?"

"Well, Sam said...," started Sandy

"Sam said not to disturb you guys, so we didn't come in," Melody finished.

"Well," I said beginning to get up. "Anybody had breakfast yet?"

"Not yet," Sam said, managing to get a word in.

"We were hopin' to have breakfast with you," piped Sandy.

"Well then," I said making to my feet with a groan. "Let's go." I put my hands out to help Molly to her feet. "You hungry?"

"Yes! I'm starving!" she said still a little wobbly.

"You gonna be alright?" I asked.

She looked around at my children and how they were taking the whole thing in stride, not even flinching at the idea that we had actually, and in fact, left the ground and took flight into the air. "Yes, I'm ok..., I feel a little silly."

"No, not at all." I kissed her. "You like hot cakes?"

"Hot..., cakes?" She asked.

I took her hand, and with kids in tow walked out the main dining hall to the corridor. "Oh, you'll love my hot cakes."

"Dad, what is she saying?" Ian asked.

"Oh, that's right! I forgot about the translators. She says she's hungry, so let's go to my quarters and have a big o' breakfast, and introduce everybody."

"Bridge to Captain."

"Yes George," I responded to my watch again.

"We're on course for Pasaris, should be there in about twelve hours."

"Slow down and make that..., oh..., four days, could you? I could use some rest and unwinding first."

"No prob. Have fun..., er..., you know what I mean."

Four days later...

"Helm, standard approach to Unarak station."

"Aye sir." Our visit to Pasaris seemed pretty routine, except for the tension that filled the bridge. George, who had given up the helm, this time, to a hologram, had taken a seat to my right and appeared very nervous. The prospect of a confrontation between the Pasarins and myself was definitely not a welcome feeling, given the fact that they were more advanced then than we were, on the order of about eighty or so years. Although there was consolation in knowing that most of their advancement was in the field of medical sciences and not in any military consideration, they were a peace loving people after all, and also in the fact that we had some advancements of our own that they did not; namely the polynesium and all that went with it, something that they had refused some years back.

"De-cloak."

"De-cloaking," Came a response.

"De-cloaking?" George asked a bit confused. "Ringing their door bell?"

"You might say that," I said trying to look as relaxed and confident as I could. As we slowly approached one the several large space stations in orbit about the planet two small craft began to advance on us.

"Scout ships sir," responded the crewman at navigation. "Two of 'em. Shields sir?"

"Keep shields down."

"What's the plan 'ol buddy." George asked, looking as if he found it harder and harder to get comfortable in his seat.

"Slow deep breaths," I told him. "It's going to be alright. I pressed a button on arm of my chair and tried my Pasarin, although it had been a while. "Unarak Station, This is Star Shark, request permission for docking."

A response came all too swift. "Star Shark, this is Flight control Unarak Station. You have clearance for docking at port six."

"Copy that, docking port six." Now back to English. "Take us in, Helm, docking port six."

"Aye sir."

"One big happy family," George's confusion was growing ever more fervent.

"Um, George, I have a confession to make."

"Oh?"

"Captain," The crewman at navigation interrupted. "A signal sir, on a private channel and scrambled."

"Now we're getting' somewhere," George said still trying to get comfortable.

I pushed a button on the arm of my chair again as a small screen beside it lit up with a familiar face. "Councilman Unarak, it's good to see you again," I said speaking in Pasarin once again.

"And you, my friend," spoke the face. "You have come to make a delivery, I presume."

"Signed, sealed and delivered."

"Wonderful, wonderful. I will see you personally at port six." I pushed the button again and the face was gone. Turning to face George, I found him leaning on his arm, staring at me with a sharp look in his eye. His stare lasted for a moment before finally voicing his current trepidation.

"How 'bout in English now," he commanded with some impatience and feeling a little lost.

"five minutes to docking," Reported the helm.

"Mister Brewman, you have the bridge," Getting up from my chair, I motioned graciously toward the door. "George?"

"Aye sir, I have the bridge," reported Brewman.

"You're not going to tell me are you?" George said leading the way down the corridor. "You always do that. You do realize how much I hate that, don't you, ol' buddy?"

"Oh no, no. I am going to tell you. In fact you'll hear even it from the horse's mouth…, really." As we continued toward the elevator George gave me a sideways look.

Stopping by to gather up Molly, the three of us made our way to down to the deck three airlock to await our guest. George appeared to be restraining his obvious irritation but held his peace by changing the subject.

"So," he asked, "did you ever find out how you and Molly are being connected mentally, or emotionally, or whatever?" Just then a dull thud was heard behind the airlock door in front of us, followed by several loud clicks. Our guests had arrived.

"Yes, actually," I said. "Well almost." Molly leaned up against me and gathered my arm. "As you know brain wave patterns are as unique as finger prints, no two people are alike. Well, as it turns out, and according to Doc, she and I have patterns that are very, very close. I mean so close that they're almost the same, and the odds of that happening are extremely infinitesimal, but, even so, still not close enough to warrant such a link as we have, or to even cause such an effect, which is technically impossible, really."

"Ok, so…, how's it happening?"

"Well, it turns out, that polynesium has a natural molecular frequency vibration, when stimulated, that's within the normal human brainwave frequency range. And because of its other natural, and very powerful, properties, and because both of us were literally bathing in it, it was bridging the gap in some mysterious way."

"Incredible."

"I mean, she was literally living right on top of all that polynesium, and me…, well I'm quite surrounded by it. The hull of this ship is made of a composite of the stuff, not to mention all of it that's stuffed in the engines. And if you remember, that's when I started having those dreams."

"Right. Incredible. Even over planetary distances. That would definitely be worth a study."

"Yeah but, that's not all. Remember when I was telling you about how my mom, when she was pregnant with me, would go and eat some of that strange plant she and Dad found by the polynesium samples they found?

"Yeah."

"Well, Molly and her people have been eating it their whole lives, using it for medicinal purposes n' stuff. Just a theory of mine. Other than that, I have no idea how that was happening. Just chock it up to the minerals other mysterious properties and who knows what other kind of other weird stuff was goin' on."

"Even with this thing in my ear I still have no idea what you just said," piped Molly.

"Well, what it means is we can blame the polynesium," I told her with a kiss.

"What it means is," she said running her finger down my face, "you can't get away with anything anymore."

"Yes dear," I said chuckling, kissing her again.

"What'd she say?" George asked.

"She said, that it means that I can't get away with anything."

George burst out with a laugh. "Now that's funny. The mystery captain is now an open book."

Just then the airlock door opened revealing the head councilmen of the Pasarin governing body along with two of his aids. Two other men, wearing some sort of battle uniform, complete with helmet and rifle type weaponry, followed behind. George being ready this time, finally put a translator in his ear.

"Councilman Unarak, you haven't changed a day," I greeted, approaching him with my hand out speaking his native language once again. "You look as good as ever. Welcome aboard".

"I'm afraid my health is not what is once was, my friend," he said taking my hand as he looked around at his new surroundings. "But I thank you anyway. My duties as head of the council has taken its toll these last few years, what with A-Meel and other things that have been happening."

"Can't be all bad, I mean having a whole space station named after you, and everything."

"My reward for ensnaring our former council member. How is Mister Me-lot anyway?"

"A little beat up, but none the worse for wear. Did you get my report I sent?" Out the corner of my eye I could see confusion, once again, beginning to build on Georges face.

"Yes I did and we owe you our gratitude, captain." Uneasiness was now coming from the councilman, as well. "I do hope you're fully recovered."

"Oh, it was, as we say on Earth, 'a piece of cake'." I Rubbed the back of my head in remembrance of the pain. I get blown up and almost die and he gets a space station named after him. "All in all, I think the whole thing came down pretty well. A thousand pardons, Councilman, where's my manners?" I held my hand out to George. "You remember George Cooper."

"Yes, we met briefly the last time you were here, Hello Mister Cooper." Councilman Unarak took George's hand and pumped it.

"Hello sir," greeted George with a bit of reservation.

"And this is Molly, from Maru…, my wife."

"Really! This is indeed a surprise, and a pleasure!" He gave her a bow. "Ooya na."

"Ooya na," she returned shyly with a curtsey.

"Congratulations Captain," said the councilman. "Rather unexpected."

"Yes…, it was." I leaned over to one of my security officers "Go and bring the prisoner."

"Yes sir." As they went, the councilman's own guards followed.

"Wait a minute, wait a minute!" burst George suddenly, waving his hands, "aren't we suppose to be mad at them or somethin'? I mean, what the heck is going on?"

"My apologies George. It was necessary to leave you out of the loop."

"What? You mean the whole thing was a ruse?"

"You see, Mister Cooper," the councilman began to explain, "we could not go after A-Mecl Me-lot ourselves. So we asked your Captain to do it for us."

"Why is that?"

"Because," I continued for the councilman. "If A-Meel knew that it was the council that was after him, he would have only dug in deeper or disappeared all together and they never would have caught him. And who knows how much more devastation he would have caused on Maru afterwards. We both knew how bad he wanted the polynesium and the technology, so we used the Shark as bate and made him come to us."

"I see," said George. "Rather risky. So why not just fill me in from the start, why all the secrecy?"

"Your reaction had to be genuine should you happen to be captured and interrogated."

"Well…, I see." George rubbed his face. "You wouldn't mind keeping me IN the loop from now on, would you?"

"I promise," I patted him on the back of the shoulder. "Councilman, how 'bout the ol' ten cent tour?"

"I would love to," he said, "your ship is a beauty, and a might larger than the last one, I might add. But I really have to be going."

"Larger and more new toys," I temped rather pridefully.

"Yes well, it's probably safer I don't know about them."

"By the way, I thought that partially built craft you had under the castle was brilliant. It actually had me going for a while there." I watched and waited for a reaction as I noticed our guest's nervousness growing stronger the more he stayed.

"Well, I'm just glad it all worked in the end and the whole thing turned out well."

Both sets of guards returned with a bound and gagged A-Meel as then he was quickly whisked off by Unarak's own officers.

"What's with the gag?" I asked.

"He was yelling and spitting, sir." responded one of my men. "As soon as we opened the holding cell he started, shouting, yelling and spitting on everyone."

"Hmmm." I turned to Molly with a big grin on my face. "Must've been the rocano fruit."

"Whaddya mean?" asked George.

"Well, Molly just happened to bring a couple of those stink oranges on board with her..." I looked at her with a sharp eye, "for who knows what reason, and I decided to offer them to A-Meel in his cell." After a brief silence the four of us burst out laughing. "Well..., It was time for his lunch. So I served him lunch." The laughing continued.

"Captain, it's been a pleasure." Councilman Unarak shook my hand once more and stepped into the airlock. "Oh, I may have another mission for you if you're interested."

"Usual fee?"

"Of course."

"I'll contact you."

Councilman Unarak bowed, then the airlock closed.

"What's the fee," asked George, as we began to walk back down the corridor toward the bridge.

"Medical technology! These people have advanced in the medical sciences like you wouldn't believe. Instead of spending millions on guns and ammo, they spend it on medical research. Rock n' roll."

"Rock n' roll," repeated Molly with a grin.

"Rock n' roll," I repeated kissing her. "But…, they're still hiding a lot, Mr. Cooper." I stopping our walk mid hallway.

"Woopes!" George's confusion returning to his face. "But you and he just told me…"

"Yes, we did and…, it was, but…, there's still too many unexplainable goings on, back on Maru, and I ain't letting go till I find out the real truth. I care deeply for these people and I'm not going to have anything happen to them."

"Like?"

"Like the holes that Molly and I almost fell to our deaths in, that were dug long before A-Meel was said to have arrived. And that half built craft."

"A plant to intice A-Meel…, yes?" George watched me shake my head. "No?"

"I wasn't suppose to find it. There's no chance in the world that the Pasarin government would ever approve the kind of expenditure that it would take to partially build a full sized starship just to retrieve some moron!" I resumed my walk down the corridor. "And there were other things. Remember that cloaked ship in orbit? That was them keepin' tabs on our progress."

"You lettin' me in on this one this time? he asked.

"Oh yes, my friend," I asured. "Oh yes."

EPILOGUE

The trip back to Earth would take about two weeks, in which I would then give the Shark a complete once over before starting out back to Maru again. Molly seemed to be adapting to life here a lot better than I had hoped as she was spending most of her time doing her best to catch up the last few hundred years. A daunting task to say the least but it was keeping her busy. She still seemed mesmerized by all the technological advancements the ship had to offer as well as the beauty and awe of her celestial surroundings outside which also seemed to keep her glued to the windows. Her fear was gone and she had no problem wandering around without the trepidation of falling off somewhere. Nanny did her best to help familiarize Molly with all the equipment in the galley as cooking was where Molly was at her absolute best, which is the way with most of the people of Maru. Eating 'real cooking' as she called it was far better than pulling something out of those magic holes in the wall. No objection here what so ever. Eating something she has made with her hands was certainly better, by far, than anything that's been reconstituted. Although this did require us to take on unique supplies now and then to provide her with all the essential elements to do so. Her knowledge with herbs combined with her unique cooking skills helped to provide us with a far healthier nutritional regime then what we were getting before.

But there still was one very important detail that had yet to be introduced to Molly. Holograms. I would try and pick a moment when she would be the most relaxed as she adapted to her new and strange environment, so as to not to scare the life out of her during such an introduction.

*   *   *   *   *   *

Earth was now seven days away and time once again for George and I's weekly sword play in our favorite game room.

"You ready for the battle of yer life Mister Cooper?" I walked up to him as he leaned on the doorway.

"Actually," he hesitated, "you have a new partner waitn' for ya."

"Oh? Who? One of the kids? I think one of 'em wanted me to start showin' 'em how. I guess now's a good time as any." The door slid open to the white padded room inside, and there standing in the middle, with sword in hand, was a single figure dressed in full sports gear suited for the mission at hand, complete with head gear totally covering the face.

"What's with the head gear?" The figure remained silent but brought their sword up at the ready. "Not gonna say anything eh?" Taking my sword off the rack I also brought it to the ready. "So who is this?" We walked around each other on our guard, gently moving our swords around looking position. "Well, yer definitely female from the way that suit is fittin'." My opponent lunged which I quickly met with a block. Then another which I barely caught that time. "Well, one thing's for sure, your good." Then suddenly one shot came after another, which I could bare keep up with, and was done with such fury as to continually keep me off my guard.

"Whoa!" I squeeled a little surprised. Without warning, I suddenly found my own sword being flipped out of my hand and into the wall. "Wow! Ok, just who is this anyway? Has to be a hologram George cooked up as a joke, cause he knows he can never beat me." It was then I heard giggling coming out from behind the mask. "Ah, no way." I reached over to the mysterious swordsman and flipped the off the helmet.

Underneath was a short, gorgeous, blue eyed blonde, just beaming. "You!" Yet again I was caught totally off my guard.

"Hey, I was born with one of these in my hand Mister Captain sir." Molly put her arms around me and held me tight. I guess there was still a lot that I didn't know about this new arrival in my life, but we had the rest of our lives to discover just what these mysteries were. And I had a feeling that from now on, it was not just her life that was going to be very different, but the adventure in mine had just begun as well.

"You're gonna keep me on my toes, aren't ya, Pretty lady?"

"Yes I am," she said "So look out mister." We stood for a moment clutching each other, tight holding each other's gaze, our minds connecting as our eyes began to water.

"Hello," I said softly.

"Good morning," she said.

CPSIA information can be obtained at www.ICGtesting.com
Printed in the USA
BVOW041811300912

301729BV00001B/50/P